Al

THE MYSTERY
OF THE SMUGGLERS' WRECK

N

Carrickstowe

Grand Vista
Hotel

Tregower
Hamlet

Sunset
Lodge

Westward
Beach

Pendragon
Manor

Quarry

SOUTH
MOOR

West Rock
Beach

Keyhole Cove

Pencarrick
Point

CASTLE
KEY

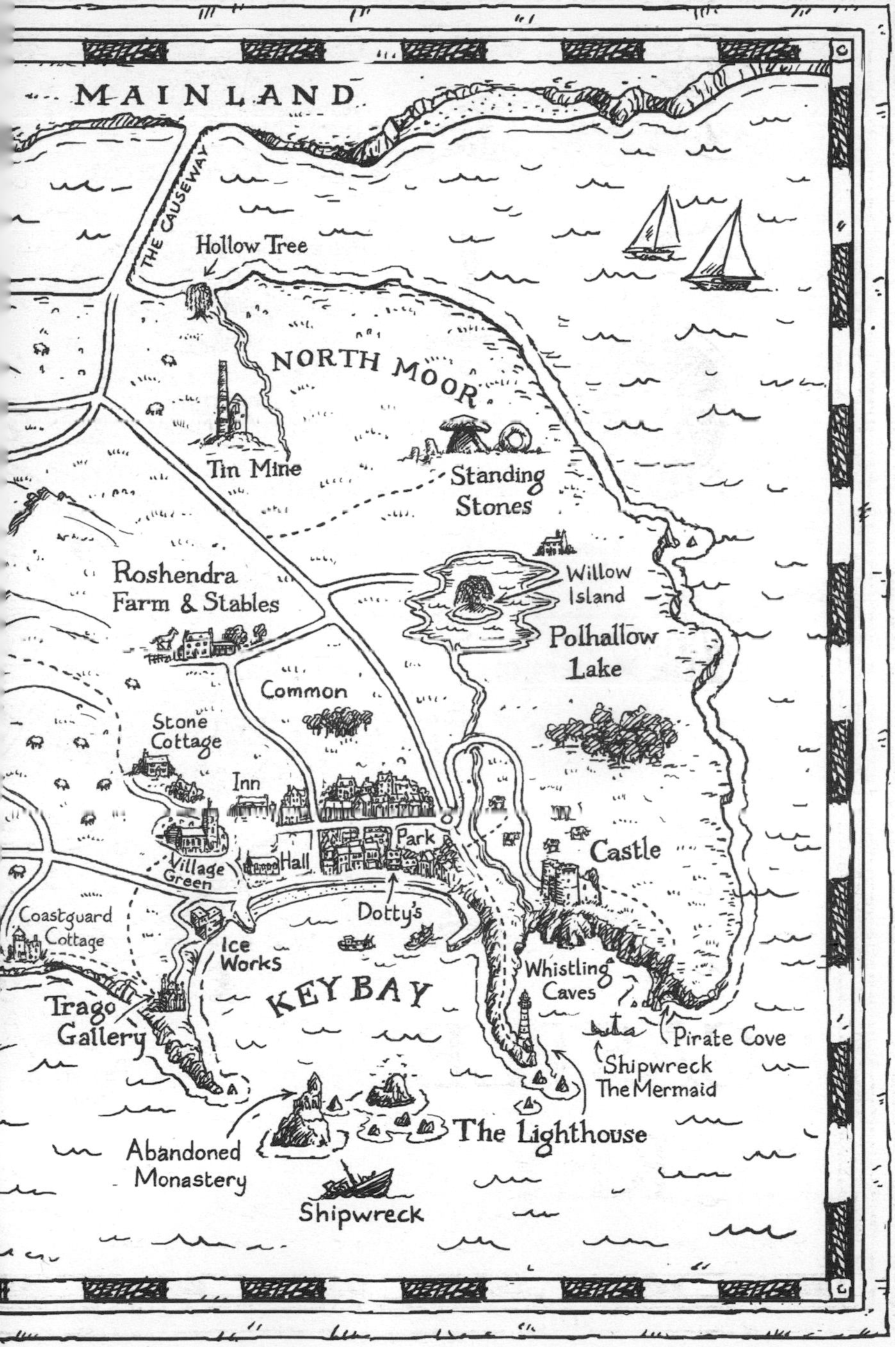
MAINLAND
THE CAUSEWAY
Hollow Tree
NORTH MOOR
Tin Mine
Standing Stones
Roshendra Farm & Stables
Willow Island
Polhallow Lake
Common
Stone Cottage
Inn
Park
Castle
Village Green
Hall
Dotty's
Coastguard Cottage
Ice Works
Whistling Caves
KEY BAY
Trago Gallery
Pirate Cove
Shipwreck The Mermaid
The Lighthouse
Abandoned Monastery
Shipwreck

Collect all the Adventure Island *books*

❏ The Mystery of the Whistling Caves

❏ The Mystery of the Midnight Ghost

❏ The Mystery of the Hidden Gold

❏ The Mystery of the Missing Masterpiece

❏ The Mystery of the Cursed Ruby

❏ The Mystery of the Vanishing Skeleton

❏ The Mystery of the Dinosaur Discovery

❏ The Mystery of the Drowning Man

☑ The Mystery of the Smugglers' Wreck

❏ The Mystery of the Invisible Spy

ADVENTURE ISLAND
THE MYSTERY OF THE SMUGGLERS' WRECK

Helen Moss

Illustrated by Leo Hartas

Orion
Children's Books

First published in Great Britain in 2012
by Orion Children's Books
a division of the Orion Publishing Group Ltd
Orion House
5 Upper St Martin's Lane
London WC2H 9EA
An Hachette UK company

1 3 5 7 9 10 8 6 4 2

A catalogue record for this book is
available from the British Library.

ISBN 978 1 4440 0535 6

Printed in Great Britain by
Clays Ltd, St Ives plc

For Amber Caravéo, Editor Extraordinaire

One

The Wreck of the *Mermaid*

'That's where the *Mermaid* ran aground.'

Emily Wild pointed out across the bay towards Pirate Cove.

Jack took the binoculars and focused on the jagged rocks jutting up from the water, rocketing the waves into fountains of white spray.

Jack and his older brother Scott had only received Emily's text message (*new guest – v. v. interesting*) half an hour ago, but they'd sprinted all the way to The Lighthouse from Stone Cottage, where they were staying with their Great-aunt Kate for the Easter holidays. Emily never gave much away in a text (in case her phone fell into enemy hands, she claimed) but the boys knew her well enough to know that *v. v. interesting* had to be something good.

Now they were all sitting on the rocks below the old red and white lighthouse, which Emily's parents ran as a Bed and Breakfast, along with Emily's little dog Drift, of course. A young man with dark, closely cropped hair and light brown skin stretched over angular cheekbones and a square jaw was waging war with a large map; every time he unfolded another section, a wilful sea breeze flipped it up over his head.

'This is Joe Gordon,' Emily said. 'He checked in at The Lighthouse this morning.'

'Hi there!' Joe peeled the flapping map from his face and waved.

'Joe is going to be diving down to the shipwreck.' Emily scooped up a handful of stones and weighted the map down on a flat rock. Drift thought this was a great game. He began picking up pebbles in his jaws and dropping them on the map.

'So, you're exploring the *Mermaid* for your research?' Scott asked. Scott and Jack's dad, Leo Carter, was an archaeologist, so they were used to people trekking off to far-flung locations to unearth bits of ancient history.

But Scott couldn't help feeling a bit disappointed. Since they'd started coming to Castle Key last summer, the guests at The Lighthouse had included an ex-SAS stunt man, a glamorous international art thief, and a group of legendary rock stars. Joe Gordon seemed a nice enough guy, but a *historian* wasn't exactly in the same league – even if he was wearing the coolest pair of trainers Scott had seen in a long time.

But Joe Gordon shook his head. 'No, it's not research exactly, I'm —'

'Joe's just started a diving company that recovers valuable cargo from shipwrecks,' Emily interrupted.

Scott was impressed. 'A *professional treasure-hunter*?'

'You mean that's actually a *job*?' Jack asked in disbelief. 'How come nobody mentioned that one at our last school careers day?'

Joe laughed. 'We've been trying to keep it a secret for years!'

'So what do you think you'll find down there?' Scott nudged aside a pile of Drift's stones and studied the map. Joe had marked the location of the wreck in red pen.

Joe rubbed his chin. 'Well, the *Mermaid's* been down there over two hundred years. She sank in —'

'1779,' Emily chipped in.

'That's right. She was a big cutter belonging to —'

'Thomas Pendragon,' Emily interrupted again. 'He was the owner of Pendragon Manor at the time.'

'Exactly,' Joe said. 'A wealthy landowner. But he was also a well-known—'

'Smuggler!' Emily breathed, her eyes shining with delight.

Joe Gordon turned to the boys and grinned. 'Is she always like this?'

Scott and Jack both nodded. 'Yeah.'

'Like *what*?' Emily interrupted.

Scott, Jack and Joe Gordon laughed.

'You haven't let Joe finish a single sentence, Em,' Scott explained.

Jack came to Emily's defence. 'She can't help it. Smuggling is one of Emily's favourite subjects. Along with espionage and criminal investigation. She's totally obsessed.'

'I am *not* obsessed!' Emily protested, raking tresses of long conker-brown hair out of her eyes. She was seriously considering giving both Scott and Jack a hefty shove. But she stopped herself. For a start, they might fall off the rocks into the sea. *And maybe they have a point,* she thought reluctantly. *I suppose I might have been bulldozing Joe a bit.* 'OK, I promise I won't butt in any more!' She laughed and mimed a lip-zipping action.

Joe Gordon smiled. 'It's OK. I don't blame you for being interested. The history of smuggling in Cornwall is fascinating. It was big business in the eighteenth century. Brandy, silver, tobacco, tea, silks . . . Most people round here were involved one way or another. It was one of the few ways to make a living.'

'And everyone hated the customs men who came to collect the taxes,' Emily added. Then she clapped her hand over her mouth. 'Oops, I'm doing it again!'

'That's alright. You go for it,' Joe said with a grin. 'You obviously know your stuff.'

'The inlets near Pirate Cove, and further west around Keyhole Cove, were perfect places to land the smuggled goods,' Emily explained, 'because only local sailors knew how to navigate the treacherous rocks. Customs boats wouldn't dare approach.'

'Tell me about it!' Jack laughed, remembering their own recent escapades saving a drowning man in Keyhole Cove. Those rocks were lethal.

'So how come the *Mermaid* ran aground if the smugglers knew their way around?' Scott asked, as logical as ever.

'Thomas Pendragon was betrayed!' Emily said dramatically. She remembered the story well. Old Bob the fisherman had told it to her many a time. 'One of the servants at Pendragon Manor had been accused of stealing from the house, so she decided to get her revenge. She found out when the *Mermaid* would next be sailing back from France, with a cargo of contraband, and she tipped off the customs men. They overpowered the smugglers' landing party – the men who were waiting to help unload – and then lay in wait at Pirate Cove to catch the smugglers as they came ashore. But one of Pendragon's men on the island heard about the ambush plan and lit a fire on the cliff near the castle to warn him.'

Jack followed Emily's gaze up to the ruined castle high on the cliff top. He could almost see the beacon burning. 'So what happened?'

'Pendragon tried to retreat but it was too late. The customs men fired on them from land and from small boats,' Emily went on. 'In all the confusion, the *Mermaid* hit the rocks and sank. All hands – including Pendragon – were drowned.'

'Wow!' Jack whistled. 'Cool story.'

He turned to Joe Gordon. 'And now you're going to salvage all the smuggled cargo from the wreck?' His imagination was running on turbo power, conjuring up an underwater Aladdin's cave of gold ingots and glittering jewels.

Joe shook his head. 'Unfortunately, there's not much left down there. There've been lots of dives over the years and anything valuable has been taken already. No, I'm looking for the body of Thomas Pendragon.'

Scott frowned. 'Surely it's just a skeleton?'

'It's what the skeleton's *wearing* that I'm interested in,' Joe said.

Jack was puzzled. 'But won't all the cloth have rotted into fish food by now?'

'I'm not after his *clothes*,' Joe explained. 'The company that now own the Pendragon Estate contacted me a few weeks ago. Their lawyers found an old letter in the library at the manor. It's from Thomas Pendragon to his son. It mentions a special compass with some kind of map or code engraved into the brass lid, revealing the secret hiding place where Pendragon and other smugglers stashed their contraband before selling it on. To this day, it's never been found.'

Secret hiding place! The thrilling words sent a shiver down Jack's spine. This story just kept getting better. 'So you're going to find the compass and *then* find the treasure?'

'That's the plan. The new owners of the Pendragon Estate have hired me to try to recover the compass for them. In the old letter, Pendragon told his son that he always wore the compass on a chain around his neck.'

Suddenly Scott noticed that they'd been talking about smuggling for two whole minutes and Emily hadn't interrupted once! 'Are you alright, Em?' he asked.

'Hmm? What?' Emily murmured. She'd hardly heard Scott's question. She was too busy gazing out towards Pirate Cove. Somewhere, far beneath those cold, deep waters, the wreck of the *Mermaid* had lain silent for hundreds of years, along with her ghostly skeleton crew and the key to a secret hoard of forgotten treasures! An idea was unfolding in Emily's mind – an idea so magical she hardly dared put it into words.

Wouldn't it be the most amazing adventure ever to be the one to find the Pendragon compass?

When she finally spoke, Emily's voice was barely more than a whisper. 'You couldn't take me down to the wreck, could you?'

Two

Serious Trouble

J oe laughed. 'I'd be happy to show you the wreck. But, of course, you'd have to be a qualified scuba diver!'

Emily could tell Joe thought *that* was about as likely as her being a brain surgeon or an Olympic shot-putter. 'Well that's alright then,' she said casually. 'We did a diving course at school last year and I got my PADI Open Water certificate.' But then she felt a tug of guilt. She was certain the boys wouldn't have learned to dive back home in London. Would it be very selfish to go off exploring the *Mermaid* if they couldn't come too?

But to Emily's astonishment, Scott was nodding enthusiastically. 'Me too!'

'Are you serious?' Emily asked.

'Yeah, last year we went to Scotland with Dad. While he was off excavating an Iron Age burial chamber on the Isle of Mull, we did a diving course.'

Emily smiled at Joe. 'Great, so when do we go?'

'We can help you search for the body, too,' Scott added. 'We'll be dead useful.'

Joe laughed. 'How could I refuse, when I'm being ambushed on all sides? I have to do a test dive first thing in the morning to make sure the wreck is safe. If I'm done in time, I could take you afterwards – if you can get permission from your parents, that is . . .'

'Thank you!' Emily whooped.

'See you tomorrow then,' Joe laughed as he folded the map and headed back to The Lighthouse.

'I'll text Dad now!' Scott was already pulling his phone from his jeans pocket.

'Well, I hope you two have *bags* of fun!' Jack said huffily. He jumped up and stalked off along the promontory.

Emily stared after him. This wasn't like Jack! Why wasn't he shouting *Awesome! What are we waiting for?* at the prospect of exploring a real-life smugglers' wreck?

'What's *his* issue?' Scott laughed. Then it came to him. Of course! They'd both completed the first five days of the PADI course, but on the last day . . .

'Jack didn't actually get his certificate,' Scott explained.

'Why not?' Emily asked.

'Someone told him they'd seen a great white shark.' Scott couldn't help grinning at the memory. 'You should have seen his face! He refused to get back in the water. The great wally! Everyone knows there are no great whites in Scotland.'

'So who told him there were, then?' Emily shot Scott a suspicious look. 'It wasn't *you*, was it?'

Scott studied his feet. It had been really funny at the time. How come he felt such a weasel about it now? 'Er, I can't really remember . . .'

Emily planted her hands on her hips. 'We can't go without him!'

'Why not?' Scott demanded. 'It's not like we're the Three Musketeers! *All for one and one for all* and all that!'

Emily looked along the promontory. Maybe Scott was right. They didn't have to do everything together. And she *really* wanted to go on that dive. But Jack looked so miserable with his hands stuffed into his pockets, kicking at clumps of heather. Drift trotted after him, then looked back, one paw raised and his spotted ear perked. He could tell something was wrong.

Suddenly Emily had an idea. She ran after Jack and grabbed his arm. 'Could you do me a big favour?' she asked.

Jack didn't stop.

'I really need someone to look after Drift for me tomorrow,' Emily persisted. 'He can't come on the dive, of course, and he'd be bored waiting in the boat by himself. Would you mind?'

Jack was so surprised he turned round. Maybe Scott hadn't told Emily about the Scottish Great White Fiasco. Then he thought again. When had Scott *ever* missed an opportunity to make out his younger brother was Wimp of the Year? Emily was just being nice, *pretending* she didn't know.

Jack shrugged. 'OK,' he muttered.

He didn't really have much choice.

—

Next morning Scott couldn't concentrate on his guitar practice, or even on watching TV. He ended up helping Aunt Kate plant out seedlings in her greenhouse. But he was so busy checking his phone for messages from Emily that he mixed up the marigolds with the marrows, and the lupins with the lettuce.

Eventually, Aunt Kate put down her trowel, looked at him over her glasses and smiled. 'Scott, dear, would you mind very much *not* helping me for a while?'

Jack rolled his eyes. 'It's only a stupid shipwreck,' he grumbled. 'Joe said there's no treasure left down there. It'll be a few planks covered in barnacles! Big deal!'

But at last Emily called.

The dive was on!

'Cheers!' Jack muttered darkly, as Scott shoved a seed tray into his hands and hared out of the greenhouse. 'I'll just go and collect Drift then, shall I?'

The seed tray slipped, tipping a small avalanche of compost down Jack's shorts.

This was turning out to be a perfect day.

⁓

Scott headed straight for the Castle Key Cabin on the seafront to hire a wetsuit and diving gear. The owner, Mrs Phillips, was away on holiday, so her assistant, Theo Jarvis – a tall, gangly surfing fanatic with a thicket of wild hair bleached by sun and sea salt – was looking after the shop. He was very knowledgeable about all the equipment for hire and soon had Scott kitted out.

Emily ran to meet Scott as he left the shop, and helped carry the cumbersome equipment down to the harbour where Joe Gordon was waiting. He'd chartered a large motorboat, *Island Mist,* to take them to the dive site, as well as a local skipper who knew the dangerous waters around Pirate Cove. Ryan Trevithick was the great-nephew of Old Bob, the Castle Key fisherman the friends knew so well. With his craggy features and old woollen cap pulled down to meet bushy eyebrows, he looked like a slightly younger clone of his great-uncle.

Emily and Scott settled down on deck and started organizing their gear; Scott wasn't surprised to see that Emily had brought along a small waterproof camera, a dive knife and an underwater notepad. She wouldn't let a detail like being on the seabed stop her having her full investigation kit at the ready. Knowing Emily, even if they didn't find Thomas Pendragon, she'd uncover a criminal gang of villainous sea urchins or a dolphin double agent.

Joe Gordon checked his watch. 'Where's Kelly got to?'

'Kelly?' Scott asked.

'Kelly Mann,' Emily told him. 'She's from Australia and she's staying at The Lighthouse too. She's diving with Joe to make a documentary film.'

'It'll be good advertising for my wreck-recovery business,' Joe added. 'We might even get on TV if we find anything good. If she ever turns up, that is.'

'There she is!' Emily pointed out a short, plump woman hurrying towards them. Kelly Mann had straight dark hair cut in a pudding-bowl style, and she wore a baggy black *Adopt a Gorilla* t-shirt over her wetsuit. 'How's it going?' she shouted in a big booming voice.

The boat rocked alarmingly as Scott helped her aboard with her dive bag and two bulky camera cases.

At last they set off. As *Island Mist* scudded across the choppy waves, Joe talked them through the dive.

'It's all pretty straightforward. The *Mermaid* lies in shallow waters. We'll only be going down to fifteen metres max. I fixed a shotline to the wreck from a surface buoy yesterday, so we'll use that to guide us down.'

'No problem,' Scott said, but his heart was starting to race. He hadn't dived for a year. Would he remember what to do?

As if reading his mind, Joe went on. 'We'll run through some emergency drills in the water to refresh everyone's memory. We'll have dive buddies of course. Scott, you stick with me, and Emily can team up with Kelly.'

Kelly high-fived Emily with a force that nearly toppled her overboard.

'And a couple of ground rules,' Joe added. 'Stay with your buddy at all times and we're not going *inside* the wreck today. You kids aren't qualified wreck divers yet. Just look from the outside.'

Emily opened her mouth as if to object but then she nodded reluctantly. She knew Joe couldn't risk them getting trapped inside the wreck.

While Ryan anchored *Island Mist* near the orange surface buoy, the four divers ran through their safety routine, checking their own equipment and then their buddy's. Scott placed the regulator in his mouth and pressed the purge valve. The hiss of air from the cylinder indicated it was all working fine. He glanced at Emily to see whether she looked as nervous as he felt. But she was grinning with excitement as she tightened the straps of her buoyancy control device – a kind of high-tech life jacket – and adjusted her weight belt.

At last the four divers hauled themselves onto the side of the boat, waddling like clowns in their diving fins. Scott clamped his hand over his facemask and regulator to hold them in place and rolled backwards into the waves. He quickly righted himself and joined the others in a circle, treading water. When they'd all signalled they were ready Joe pointed his thumb down at the water. It was time to descend.

With fumbling fingers Scott let out some air from his buoyancy control device. Within a few moments he was sinking, feeling his way down the guide rope. Blood roared in his ears. At first his lungs fought to gulp down air. *This is all wrong!* they screamed. *Humans can't breathe underwater!* But then his brain kicked in, reminding him to breathe slowly and deeply. He felt a squeaky sensation in his ears – like being in a plane – and remembered to hold his nose and breathe out to equalize the pressure. His ears popped. That felt better! He was starting to relax now.

Joe Gordon glided in front of him, trailed by a stream of air bubbles. *Are you OK?* he signalled.

Scott made an O with his index finger and thumb to signal *OK*.

Soon the shadowy bulk of the *Mermaid* loomed into view. Resting on its side, partly embedded in sand, the huge wooden hull towered up like a wall. With slow, steady kicks, the group of divers swam along its length. Kelly held her video camera out in front of her, its lights sticking out on either side like insect eyes on stalks. They illuminated the fish – Emily recognized blennies and wrasse – nibbling among the marine plants and crustaceans that furred the old hull. Miniature rainforests of straggling sea fans and pale dead men's fingers waved as if beckoning her closer. But Emily wasn't interested in corals. She was hoping to see some *real* dead men's fingers.

They rounded the bow of the ship, splintered by its impact with rock or seabed, to see the mast rising up through the water from the steeply tilted deck. Ropes and ribbons of sailcloth still clung to the rigging, wafting forlornly in the current.

While Scott and Joe began marking out a search grid on the seabed with orange pegs, Emily and Kelly swam closer to the deck. Here and there the woodwork had caved in to leave gaps and crevices.

If only I could slip through one of the holes and have a scout around, Emily thought. Surely Thomas Pendragon's body would be inside the wreck, not out here in the open, where there were only a few scattered flagons and chests and bits of wood. But she'd promised Joe she wouldn't go in.

25

Kelly slotted her camera through a hole in the deck near the base of the mast.

She must be getting some footage of the interior, Emily figured.

Now Kelly had poked her head and shoulders through too. Just a round black bottom and short legs stuck out, her fins paddling up and down to hold her position steady. She looked like a seal flapping its flippers as it hauled itself onto rocks, Emily thought. In fact, Kelly seemed to be doing rather a lot of flapping. Why *was* she kicking so hard?

Kelly was an experienced diver but her legs were definitely *panicking*. They were thrashing around like an Irish dancer gone berserk.

All of a sudden, Emily realized Kelly must be in serious trouble.

Three

The Jaws of Death

Emily knew she had to act fast.

She grabbed hold of Kelly's legs and tugged. Kelly kicked out, almost catching Emily in the face with her fin. But her bottom didn't budge.

Emily pulled again, even harder.

It was no good. Kelly Mann was stuck fast in the gap.

Emily swung round and shone her torch through the cloudy water. Joe and Scott were dark shapes in the distance, heads down as they worked like a pair of big fish feeding on the seabed. She tugged at the elastic strap of her tank banger. The plastic ball snapped against the metal air cylinder with a boom. Joe looked up but he was so far away there was no time to wait for his help.

Emily's heart began to pound, her lungs to squeeze, her brain to spin.

Remember your emergency drills, she yelled at herself. *What's the first rule?*

Stop, breathe, think!

She stopped, she breathed, she thought.

She couldn't pull Kelly out from this side, so she was going to have to go inside to reach her. It would mean breaking Joe's rule but this was an emergency. Kelly was her dive buddy, after all! She spotted a small hole near the stern and swam towards it. Grasping the crumbling wooden edges, she eased through to the dark interior.

The water was colder here, out of reach of the sun's filtered rays. Strange creaks and clangs echoed all around. Shining her torch beam into the blackness, Emily felt her way along as fast as she could. If Kelly's air supply wasn't working, every second was crucial.

She glimpsed movement above her head and looked up. A pair of glassy eyes stared back at her. For a moment, Emily thought she'd found Kelly. But an enormous conger eel slid out from its hideyhole and glided under her with a pulse of its muscular tail. Emily shuddered and fought back the urge to turn around and flee the wreck. Unseen creatures brushed against her bare hands. She imagined jellyfish tentacles and catfish whiskers and the bony fingers of long-dead smugglers.

Suddenly she thought she heard a banging noise over the heartbeat in her ears, but the water distorted the sound so she couldn't tell where it came from. She searched with her torch beam and finally made out Kelly's face up ahead, her terrified eyes bulging behind her mask.

The video camera was hanging from the strap around Kelly's neck. The lights had gone out and her regulator was dangling from its pipe beneath her chin.

Emily kicked hard and propelled herself forward. Kelly had seen the torchlight and was now jerking her head in distress. Air bubbles streamed from her mouth.

Emily's mind raced. What was wrong? Why hadn't Kelly put the regulator back in her mouth? Or used the back-up device if the regulator was blocked?

Then she saw the problem: Kelly's hands were entangled in a knotted mass of fishing line that was caught up on an iron hook. In the struggle to free herself, she must have accidentally knocked her regulator out of her mouth. Now she was trapped like a bluebottle in a spider's web.

In one swift move, Emily grabbed the second-stage air supply from her own cylinder and inserted it into Kelly's mouth. Then she held the woman's shoulders firmly and signalled to her to calm down. Gradually

Kelly stopped spluttering and gulping for air and began to breathe steadily.

Next, Emily inspected Kelly's regulator. To her relief there was a jet of bubbles when she pressed the purge valve. It was working fine. She nodded to Kelly, then quickly did the swap. Once Kelly was breathing from her own air supply again, Emily turned her attention to the fishing line which was wound so tightly it was sectioning Kelly's fingers into fat little sausages.

Emily pulled her knife from the quick-release sheath strapped to her leg and slid its tip carefully under the fishing line. Cutting away the bonds without nicking Kelly's skin was a painstaking task – like trying to unpick a piece of delicate lace – but at last Kelly was free. She shook her hands, which were still criss-crossed with red lines, smiled, and then gave Emily an OK sign. Emily grasped Kelly's shoulders and pushed. With much wriggling and writhing, Kelly was able to work her hips loose and all at once she shot backwards in a great jet of water and bubbles.

The whole wreck trembled, as if rocked by a distant earthquake.

Emily was following Kelly out through the gap when she felt something hard fall against her legs. She twisted round to look. A section of the deck had collapsed, trapping her by the feet.

Only a few metres away, Scott was totally unaware of Emily's solo rescue mission. He was having a less eventful time, sticking little orange plastic pegs in the sand at regular intervals. He admired Joe's logic – it was important to set up a systematic search for Pendragon's skeleton, which Joe believed lay buried beneath the sand and seaweed – but this was bordering on the obsessive. If they kept this up, they'd have the ocean pegged out all the way to Land's End.

A crab scuttled out from under a rock and looked up at him. Scott was sure it rolled its eyes.

Finally Joe looked up. He checked the dive computer he wore like an oversized watch on his wrist. He tapped it, then pointed towards the wreck and then upwards. Scott understood. They'd join Kelly and Emily for a look at the wreck, then it was time to surface. But as they approached the *Mermaid*, Scott realized there was no sign of the other two. Joe turned back to Scott and signalled that they should look around for them.

As Scott swam back to search near the mast he was almost bowled into a backflip by something bursting out from the deck. The high-speed launch whipped up such a mushroom cloud of bubbles and bits of algae and sand and seaweed that Scott couldn't make out what it was at first. The creature was big – sleek and black, with long flippers at the back. Was it some kind of marine mammal? Did seals venture this deep? Could it be a dolphin or a porpoise?

Then he saw the air cylinder.

Scott struggled not to laugh. Laughing underwater was never a good plan! It *was* a marine mammal. One called Kelly Mann, native to the tropical reefs of Australia, but an occasional visitor to Cornish waters.

Now Emily was swimming out through the hole behind Kelly. Scott was gobsmacked. How come Kelly had allowed Emily to explore *inside* the wreck? That was just so unfair! Now Emily would be going on about all the wonders she'd witnessed – while he'd seen nothing more than a million orange pegs, a sarcastic crab and a human porpoise.

Scott hovered, waiting for Emily to return to the guide rope with him, but for some reason, she stopped halfway out of the hole. He tapped his watch and pointed upwards to signal *Hurry up!* They'd already stayed underwater longer than planned and would risk running out of air soon. Emily gave him a look that, even behind the facemask, Scott could read as *Tell me something I don't know!* She twisted her body round as if trying to touch her toes. Then she straightened up and pointed frantically towards her feet, which remained out of sight inside the wreck.

Scott poked his head through the hole and shone his torch around. Now he could see what was wrong. A thick plank of wood had fallen from above, trapping Emily's feet against the lower edge of the hole. Scott reached in and tried to shift the plank, but the mighty beam wasn't going anywhere.

Scott checked his dive computer. Only fifty bars of air left. Emily couldn't have much more than that. Icy worms of fear began to writhe in his stomach. He had to find a way to free Emily before they both ran out of oxygen.

Suddenly he had an idea. It was so simple he couldn't believe he hadn't thought of it before. He reached in and felt for Emily's feet. Good: her heels were sticking out from under the plank. He grasped the nearest one, located the strap that attached the fin to her foot, and tugged it hard. It was an awkward manoeuvre at a tricky angle, but with a superhuman effort he was able to work the strap over Emily's heel. Moments later, Emily had wriggled her foot out of the fin. Scott began work on the second foot. At last the strap snapped and Emily was able to swim free, leaving behind two empty fins, trapped under the plank.

Scott was about to swim after her when he felt a nudge on his shoulder. He turned, expecting to see Emily telling him she needed help to swim without her fins.

But it wasn't Emily.

He was looking straight into a huge gaping mouth, bristling with needle-sharp teeth.

Shark!

Scott paddled very slowly back towards the hole, his

eyes never leaving the spine-chilling jaws of death.

Shark! Shark! Shark! The word pumped through his body with every heartbeat.

I know what this is, Scott thought. *It's my punishment for winding Jack up about the Scottish great white!*

In his head, he began to make frantic deals with the shark. *Please don't eat me! I promise, if I get out of this I'll never tease Jack about sharks again. OK, I'll never tease him about* anything *again. I'll be the best brother in the world . . .*

The shark stared back from small, menacing eyes. Then it snapped its jaws shut.

Scott shot back through the hole into the wreck, praying that he was taking all his limbs with him.

Then he felt something close around his leg.

Four

A Tough Job

I'm *being eaten alive by a shark!* Scott panicked. Then, *Hang on a minute!* he thought. It didn't feel like shark teeth ripping into his flesh. It felt like a human hand tugging him out of the hole.

He opened his eyes and saw Joe Gordon.

And hang on another minute! Since when were there man-eating sharks in Cornwall anyway?

Scott kicked away from Joe's grip and backed into

the hole in the deck. He just needed a moment. He couldn't let the others see him looking this shaken. And at least he'd have one quick glimpse inside the wreck before leaving.

That's when he saw the skeleton hanging upside down just above his head.

Scott swept his torch beam over the pale dome of the skull. Small silver fish darted in and out of its eye sockets. Above that loomed a bulging rib cage and a cracked pelvis, which had become caught on a hook. One arm dangled down as if to welcome Scott aboard. The other was missing.

The skeleton must have fallen through from somewhere higher up inside the deck when the plank gave way, Scott figured.

The skull bobbed as if nodding in agreement.

Scott shrank back in fear. *It's alive!* Then he realized it was just the movement of the water.

He noticed a small object dangling in front of the skull's nose cavity. It appeared to be on a chain around the skeleton's neck. Scott reached out for it, but he was too late.

Joe was already hauling him out by the ankle.

——

Meanwhile, Jack was having a rather less adrenalin-packed morning. First he cycled to The Lighthouse to collect Drift. Crumbs of compost from the seed tray had found their way into his trainers and mashed uncomfortably into his socks as he pedalled. What was he supposed to do all day while Emily and Scott were off playing *Dora the Explorer*? That's what he wanted to know! Even the weather was out to get him; a bank of thick cloud had parked itself right on top of the island.

At least Drift seemed happy to see him.

'I don't know what you're wagging your tail about, mate,' Jack grumped, ruffling Drift's ears. 'I'm the useless twerp who's afraid of sharks, remember?'

Drift didn't mind. He licked Jack's knees.

Jack couldn't help laughing. *At least dogs know the meaning of the word* loyalty, he thought. That gave him an idea. 'We don't need those two, do we, Drifty?' he said, grinning. 'Let's go and see some of our *real* friends.'

⌒

Halfway to Roshendra Farm the clouds opened. Jack pedalled as fast as he could, rain slicking his hair into his eyes and plastering his t-shirt to his body. Drift hunkered down in his special basket on the back, which Jack had borrowed from Emily's bike.

At least we'd have wetsuits on if we were diving, Jack thought gloomily as he propped his bike against the gate.

But he couldn't help smiling when two enormous

Dobermans came bounding into the yard, raindrops flying from their sleek black coats, their paws skidding on the wet concrete as they took a sharp corner.

'Tyson! Rambo!' Jack called. The dogs hurtled towards him. Jack remembered the first time he'd met these fearsome beasts. He'd thought he was about to be turned into Pedigree Chum! That was during Operation Dinosaur in the Christmas holidays, when the Dobermans still belonged to their previous owner, a bullying security guard. Now he knew that the worst he had to fear was drowning in a bucket-load of slobber. The Dobermans clearly remembered Jack; Rambo planted his paws on his shoulders and licked his chin, while Tyson butted his knees with his huge head.

The door of the farmhouse opened. Jack instantly detected cooking smells wafting out from the kitchen. He was getting sugar, vanilla, chocolate . . . When it came to the sweet stuff, his nose was almost as finely tuned as Drift's. Mrs White stood in the doorway, leaning on her walking stick. She was wearing a long white apron and a hair net covered her short grey hair. She laughed to see Jack and Drift rolling around with the Dobermans in a mass bear-hug-slash-rugby-scrum.

'Come on in out of the rain!' she called.

While Drift and the Dobermans headed off on a squirrel-hunting mission in the orchard, Jack dried out in front of the fireplace with the help of a fluffy towel and a mug of hot chocolate. Mrs White stirred an enormous copper cauldron on the stove. 'Fudge,' she said. 'I'm making a big batch for the farmers' market in Carrickstowe.' She scooped a huge wodge from the pan with a wooden paddle and walloped it down onto the kitchen table, where a marble slab had been placed ready. Using a palette knife she began to smooth the fudge out over the cold surface. 'It's Chocolate Caramel Swirl,' she said wiping her hands down her apron. 'If only I had someone to help taste it.'

Jack stared at Mrs White in disbelief. Was she actually *serious*? Finally his day was starting to look up! He volunteered and took a bite.

'Hmmm, brilliant,' he said with his mouth full. 'Although I'd better try a bit more to check that it's . . . er . . . cooked evenly.'

'Have you got time to stay and help with another batch?' Mrs White asked.

Jack pretended to check his watch. 'Yeah, I think I can spare a few minutes!'

Professional fudge-taster. Now there was *another* option that their careers teacher had forgotten to mention.

It was a tough job but someone had to do it!

As they stirred cream and sugar into the cauldron, Mrs White asked where Scott and Emily were. Jack explained about the dive to the *Mermaid*. He left out the bit about the Scottish Great White Fiasco. After all, Mrs White didn't need to know that he'd failed to get his diving certificate thanks to his stupid brother winding him up about man-eating sharks. 'I volunteered to look after Drift. I'm not that fussed about scuba diving. It's over-rated if you ask me.'

Mrs White smiled. 'Quite right! If God had meant us to swim underwater he'd have given us gills. Give me a warm kitchen any day!'

As Jack sampled his way through the entire range of fudge flavours, Mrs White chatted. She knew all about Thomas Pendragon and the wreck of the *Mermaid*. Her family had lived on Castle Key for generations and all the old smuggling stories had been passed down over the years. She explained how the government had placed massive taxes on all kinds of goods in the eighteenth century – mainly to fund the war with France – which was why so many people took up smuggling, or at least turned a blind eye to it.

'The smugglers dug so many tunnels,' she said, 'that the whole island is like a sponge! But it was always rumoured that Pendragon's hiding place was somewhere on the Pendragon Estate itself. You know all the stories about the manor being haunted?'

Jack nodded. *How could I forget?* Hiding in the wardrobe at the manor, in the attic haunted by the midnight ghost, had been one of his All-Time Top Ten Scariest Moments.

'Well, most of those rumours were put about just to keep the revenue men from coming too close,'

Mrs White said. 'If they came sniffing round and saw suspicious lights coming and going, they'd be told that it was ghosts on the prowl. Of course, it was really the smugglers bringing back new consignments of goods under cover of night.'

Jack grinned. 'So they were pretty clever at getting away with it then?'

'Oh, yes,' Mrs White said, slapping another mound of fudge onto the slab. 'And Thomas Pendragon was the wiliest one of all! He's almost as famous round here as the Carters of Prussia Cove on the mainland.'

'The Carters of Prussia Cove,' Jack repeated. 'Carter's my surname. Who were they?'

Mrs White smiled. 'Maybe they were your ancestors then. They were one of the biggest smuggling families in Cornwall.'

Jack paused with a piece of fudge mid-way to his mouth. *Cool!* He thought. *I'm descended from smugglers!* He pictured himself sailing stormy seas, dragging barrels of brandy up a beach by moonlight, and diving into a tunnel to evade the customs men.

Arrr, Jack Carter, Master Smuggler! he said to himself in his best pirate accent.

It definitely had a ring to it!

Five

Close Encounters

After the dive, Scott and Emily met up with Jack and Drift for lunch at Dotty's Tea Rooms on the seafront. The sun had finally made it through the clouds, so they took their fish and chips outside. The air was still a little chilly so none of the other tables on the pavement were taken, but Scott spotted Theo Jarvis at the Castle Key Cabin next door, wheeling out display racks of beach towels and surf boards in the hope of a sunny afternoon.

'Did you see that massive basking shark?' Emily asked, reaching for the salt and vinegar.

'Yeah, I couldn't exactly miss it,' Scott replied airily. 'I could practically see its tonsils.'

'So that's why you looked so petrified when you came out of the wreck!' Emily laughed.

'Petrified?' Scott leaned back in his chair and grinned. 'Yeah, right! Like I'm going to be scared of a *basking* shark. What's it going to do to me? Mistake me for a bit of plankton and filter-feed me to death? You'd have to be a . . .' Scott was about to score a point off Jack, but then he remembered the deal he'd made when he was staring into the jaws of death. 'I mean, well, all sharks can look a bit scary at first glance. It's understandable that some people are frightened of them.'

Jack shot his brother a searching look. The words *shark* and *scary* had come up in the same sentence, yet Scott hadn't even *mentioned* the Scottish Great White Fiasco! Was he ill or something? Come to think of it, Jack wasn't actually feeling on top form himself. He might have *slightly* overdone it in the fudge department! He looked down at his plate: two battered sausages and a mountain of chips all smothered in ketchup. He nibbled a chip then put it back. It was a tragedy of epic proportions, but his stomach was saying *no vacancies*.

He offered a sausage to Drift, who was more than happy to help out. Then he pushed the plate across the table. Emily and Scott both stared at him and then at each

44

other. This was the first recorded instance in history of Jack giving away food without threats of violence. They tucked in before he could change his mind. Diving was very hungry work – especially when it involved heroic rescue missions.

'You should have seen Joe's face when we first surfaced,' Scott told Jack. 'He was furious with us for disregarding his rules and going inside the wreck.'

Emily laughed. 'But then Kelly jumped in and explained how she'd got all caught up in that fishing line when she'd put her camera through the hole in the deck.'

'Like a total gumby!' Scott said, mimicking Kelly's Australian accent and taking up the story again. 'Next thing I know I'm all wrapped up like a Christmas parcel and I'm wedged in that bloomin' hole by the derriere. And to top it all,' Scott's imitation went on, 'I only knocked my regulator out of my mouth while I was trying to pull my hands free. I was tied up, stuck like a cork in a bottle *and* out of air. I'd have been a goner if it wasn't for my bud, Em, here.' Scott threw his arm around Emily to demonstrate Kelly's actions.

Emily grinned. 'Yeah, she practically pulverized my shoulder blades in that hug!'

Scott suddenly realized he was cuddling Emily and hastily dropped his arm before Jack noticed. 'Anyway, by the time we got back to Castle Key harbour,' he said quickly, 'Joe had heard the full story. He soon changed his tune. He said Emily had saved Kelly's life.'

Although Joe hadn't heard quite *the full story,* Scott thought, as he finished his fish and chips. In all the fuss about Kelly's rescue, Scott hadn't mentioned that the eyeball-to eyeball moment with the basking shark hadn't been his *only* close encounter on the *Mermaid.* Now he placed his knife and fork neatly together on his plate and looked slowly from Emily to Jack and then back again, making the most of the moment.

'What's up?' Jack asked. 'You got indigestion or something? You shouldn't have pigged down all my chips!'

Scott ignored him. 'You're never going to *believe* what I saw inside the wreck,' he announced.

'You mean that monster conger eel?' Emily asked with a shudder. 'I saw it too!'

Scott shook his head. 'I saw Thomas Pendragon!'

'Of course you did!' Jack snorted. 'I bet you had a swig of rum and a ship's biscuit with Blackbeard and Captain Jack Sparrow while you were down there as well.'

Emily grinned. She thought Scott was winding them up too, but then she saw his face. Beneath his floppy fringe his green eyes were deadly serious. 'Where?' she asked.

Scott gave a blow-by-blow account of how he'd seen the skeleton dangling above him inside the deck.

Emily stated at him with a mixture of wonder and

jealousy. 'How do you know it was Pendragon? Did you see the compass?'

Scott nodded. 'There was something hanging round his neck.'

'Wow!' Emily breathed. 'What did it look like?'

'Flat, roundish, about this big.' Scott indicated the size of a cricket ball with his hands. 'That's all I can tell you. Joe pulled me out before I could get a proper look.'

Buzzing with excitement, Emily grabbed her notebook from her bag and began quizzing Scott about the exact location and position of the skeleton.

Jack was starting to feel left out. 'Well, I had an interesting morning too,' he said.

Emily glanced up from her notes. 'Did you?' she murmured vaguely. She turned to Scott. 'OK. What was the compass made of?'

Scott frowned. 'I don't know. It was all sort of cased in a crust of hard sand . . .'

'Mrs White told me loads of stuff about smugglers,' Jack persisted. 'Like me and Scott could have smuggling genes.'

'Smuggling *jeans*?' Scott scoffed. 'What are you on about?'

'*Genes*, not *jeans*!' Jack snapped. 'We may be descended from a famous line of smugglers – the Carters of Prussia Cove. We're like one of those Mafia families or something.'

'Yeah, right!' Scott laughed. 'What's the probability that we're the *same* Carter family? There are six other Carters at our school and we're not related to any of them!'

'It *is* a pretty common name,' Emily agreed, returning to her notes. 'Now, we need to talk to Joe about another dive as soon as possible. We've *got* to get a better look at the compass.'

'Hello-o!' Jack said, waving his hands in front of Emily's face. 'Have I suddenly ceased to exist or something?'

'Ooh, here he is now!' Emily sprang out of her chair and waved to Joe who was walking towards them along the seafront. When he stopped to chat to Ryan Trevithick who was working on *Island Mist* in the harbour nearby, Emily couldn't contain her impatience. She ran and dragged him over to their table. Between them, Emily and Scott poured out the story of Scott's amazing find.

Emily thrust her notebook under Joe's nose. 'I've made diagrams and everything.'

Joe laced his fingers together and placed them under his chin in thought. 'Why didn't you say anything about this before?'

'You were so busy making sure Kelly and Emily were OK I didn't get a chance,' Scott explained.

Joe frowned. 'It's easy for your mind to play tricks on you underwater.'

'Yeah,' Jack muttered. 'I bet Scott imagined the whole thing,'

'I know what I saw!' Scott insisted.

'And the object hanging round the skeleton's neck was definitely *circular*, you say?' Joe asked.

'Yeah, a flattish sort of a disc.' But as Scott spoke he suddenly started to doubt himself. He closed his eyes, trying to picture the compass. He'd only glimpsed it for a moment, swaying gently in front of the skull, as if someone were trying to hypnotize Thomas Pendragon. The disc was all crusted and rough, rounded off at the edges. *Edges?* Of course! That's what had made him unsure about the shape. The compass had edges like a fifty-pence piece. 'It was a hexagon!' he exclaimed.

Joe gave Scott a searching look. 'A hexagon? Are you sure it had six sides?'

Scott nodded. 'Well, I *was* upside down underwater in the dark with a shark in my face at the time. I wasn't really counting! It might have been an octagon, I suppose.'

Joe jumped out of his chair and pumped the air with both hands. 'Jackpot!' he cried.

Six

A Shock at Pirate Cove

Joe Gordon placed both hands on the table and leaned over as if he'd been punched in the stomach. Emily was worried for a moment, but when Joe looked up he was grinning as if he'd just won the lottery on a rollover week. Without a word, he sat down, pulled his laptop from his shoulder bag and opened up a file. Scott and Emily leaned in closer to see the scanned image of a tattered old document. The ink had faded to a muddy brown but the old-fashioned handwriting, with its loops and flourishes, was still clear.

'This is Thomas Pendragon's letter to his son,' Joe explained. 'The one I told you about. Look at this line!' He pointed to the screen.

Emily did her best to decipher the elaborate script. '. . . *a fine eight-sided compost* – no, sorry – *eight-sided* compass, *worked in brass and silver*,' she read aloud.

'Eight sided!' Scott exclaimed. 'That means it was octagonal.'

'Thanks for clearing that up for us, Einstein!' Jack snapped. He was well and truly fed up with being ignored.

'Exactly,' Joe said. 'I didn't dare to believe that you'd really stumbled across Pendragon's body. But now I'm convinced. You couldn't have known the compass was octagonal unless you'd actually seen it. Well done!'

Emily began stuffing her notes back into her bag. 'We could be kitted up to dive again in half an hour . . .'

'Hold on!' Joe threw up his hands. 'We can't dive this afternoon. That's what I was just talking to Ryan about. The afternoon tide means the currents are too strong.'

Emily's face fell. Then she brightened again. 'First thing tomorrow morning. It'll be light by six.'

Joe laughed. 'You don't give up, do you? But I'm

afraid tomorrow morning I've got a group of American tourists booked in. I'm charging for guided diving tours of the wreck to help fund the project.'

Joe looked at Scott and Emily's crestfallen expressions. 'Here's what I'll do. While I'm with the Americans I'll check the compass is still there. But I promise I won't touch it. We'll all dive down together later in the morning and Kelly can film us all finding the compass together. It'll make a great scene for her documentary.'

Emily thought the plan was perfect. She high-fived with Joe and Scott. It was all *so* exciting! They'd soon have the compass and then they'd have the secret to finding the smugglers' hiding place. Would it be a map, she wondered, or a set of coded directions, or even a riddle? She couldn't wait to find out.

Jack, meanwhile, was less impressed. He was going to be left out yet again.

He almost wished Scott had never seen the crummy compass.

—

The next morning, Emily was too impatient to wait for Joe Gordon to return from his dive with the American tourists to find out whether he'd seen the compass. She insisted they all row out to Pirate Cove in her little boat, *Gemini*, to meet him there the moment he surfaced.

Perched on the rocks that surrounded the little half-moon beach, Emily trained her binoculars on the orange buoy near Ryan Trevithick's motorboat, waiting for the group to come up from the wreck.

At last she spotted the dark sleek heads beginning to pop up out of the water like a family of seals. She waved wildly to attract Joe's attention. 'I think he's seen us!'

Sitting next to her, Scott was playing it cool but deep down he was so wound up he'd not been able to eat the scrambled eggs Aunt Kate had made for breakfast. He grabbed the binoculars for a look. Then he remembered his *Be Nice to Jack* pledge to the shark. 'They've surfaced,' he called to his brother. 'Come and see!'

But Jack shrugged his shoulders and continued sulking quietly in the background. He'd almost refused to come on this stupid Compass Quest, but Emily had wanted to bring Drift and he didn't fancy being Billy-No-Mates all morning.

Scott gave up and returned to the binoculars. The divers had clambered aboard Ryan's motorboat. Kelly and the tourists were all sitting around removing their masks and air cylinders. Meanwhile, Joe was climbing into the little inflatable tender. He pulled the cord to start the outboard motor and then he was zipping over the waves to the beach.

'Here he comes!' Scott cried.

Emily jumped up, hopping from foot to foot. 'I can't wait!'

Together they ran into the shallows to help pull the tender onto the beach.

'Did you see the skeleton?' Scott asked, before Joe was even out of the water.

'Yes, hanging upside down, just as you predicted.'

Emily was taken aback. She'd expected Joe to be all fired up with enthusiasm, but his voice was strained and flat. And his square jaw was rigid.

'The compass? Did you see it?' she asked anxiously.

Joe Gordon suddenly let the tender drop onto the sand. He straightened up and marched up the beach. Scott and Emily ran after him.

Halfway to the rocks Joe stopped and turned round. 'Oh, yeah, I saw the compass alright.' He fished in the waterproof bag on his belt and held out a closed fist.

Scott and Emily exchanged bewildered glances. If Joe had found the compass why did he look as if he'd just got a parking ticket *and* been wheel-clamped?

Joe Gordon opened his hand.

Lying on his smooth brown palm was a compass. A small round green plastic compass on a length of damp elastic.

The flimsy arrow quivered. It wasn't even pointing north.

This compass certainly held no clues to the location of

the smugglers' hoard. Only the words *Scooby-Dooby-Doo, Where Are You?* stamped around the rim, and a picture of Scooby-Doo and Shaggy running across the middle. It looked as if it had come out of a Christmas cracker.

Joe narrowed his eyes at Scott. 'Is this your idea of a joke?'

Scott shook his head, barely able to speak. 'But that's not it!' he croaked. 'The compass I saw was really old. It was all crusted up . . .'

Joe sighed. 'Yeah, it's called concretion. That's what this *would* look like if it had been down there for hundreds of years. This thing's obviously not been in the water more than a couple of days.'

Emily stared at the toy compass. She hardly dared think it, but had Scott made a mistake? Coming face to face with a big shark – even a harmless one – could mess with your mind. 'Are you *sure* this isn't what you saw?' she asked him gently.

Scott's mouth dropped open. He couldn't have looked more stunned if Scooby-Doo had cruised past on a surf board.

Emily felt terrible for doubting him. 'Sorry,' she mumbled. 'It's just so weird. I don't get it.'

'Well, *I* get it!' Joe snapped. 'You two thought you'd play a little prank and *pretend* you'd found the compass!'

'What about the eight sides?' Scott stammered. 'You

said yourself I couldn't have known that—'

'You must have sneaked a look at my notes somehow.' Joe turned and started walking back to the tender.

'No way!' Scott and Emily called after him.

Jack looked up from the rocks where he'd been throwing sticks for Drift. He'd heard the whole thing. He had to admit he'd secretly felt a tiny ripple of satisfaction when Joe first said the compass was a dud. Serve Scott right for making such a song and dance about it! But now Joe Gordon was going too far. He was accusing Scott of lying. And he was clearly barking up the wrong tree. Scott didn't do *pranks*! He considered them to be *immature* (unlike Jack, who thought they were hilarious). Scott just wouldn't have the imagination to cook up something as wacky as planting a Scooby-Doo compass round a skeleton's neck.

Jack knew his brother better than anyone in the world. Yes, Scott had been boring and smug and irritating about finding that compass. But he definitely hadn't been lying about it.

And as for Emily? She'd *never* joke about smuggling! It was her one true love!

Jack ran down the beach. 'Hey! Stop!' he yelled, wading into the water after Joe. 'If my brother said there was a crusty old eight-sided compass down there, then there *was*!'

Drift joined Jack, standing up to his shoulders in the

surf to add some warning barks of his own. He didn't know what all this was about. Joe had seemed like a decent sort of human (he'd given Drift his leftover bacon rinds at breakfast), but he'd raised his voice at Emily and made her ears droop. Drift wasn't going to stand for that.

Joe looked up from starting the outboard motor. 'I admire your loyalty, but how do you explain *this*?'

He flicked the Scooby-Doo compass into the air with his thumb.

Jack opened his mouth, but Joe didn't wait for an answer. He was already roaring off so fast that the front of the tender reared up out of the waves.

Jack caught the compass and stuffed it in his shorts pocket.

The friends had rowed *Gemini* almost all the way back to the promontory before anyone broke the silence. Scott leaned on the oars and held his head in his hands. He'd never felt so humiliated in his life. It was as if a giant foot had descended from the sky and squashed him flat.

'I just don't understand it,' he muttered.

Jack grinned. 'Admit it! Your brain's finally blown a fuse and you've started seeing things!'

Scott scooped water with one of his oars and drenched

his brother in a cold shower. 'I'm *not* seeing things.'

'OK,' Jack laughed. 'A big fish ate it. Maybe that shark you saw? Like the crocodile in *Peter Pan* that swallowed an alarm clock.'

Emily rolled her eyes. 'And this shark also left the Scooby-Doo compass behind in its place, did it?' She shook her head. 'No. It's obvious, isn't it? The Pendragon compass has been stolen!'

Seven

A Brand New Investigation

After tying *Gemini* up in the little inlet on the promontory, Scott, Jack, Emily and Drift returned to The Lighthouse. But there they found a very grumpy Joe Gordon prowling around the guest lounge, so they ran up to the kitchen, threw together a packed lunch and headed straight back out again. They drifted up to the castle on the cliff top, and settled down in the ruined tower that had served as their HQ in their very first case together.

It was a good place to talk without being overheard. And a great place to plan an investigation.

'You think the compass has been stolen?' Jack snorted. 'Who by? A catfish burglar?' He laughed at his own joke but neither Scott nor Emily joined in.

'Em's right,' Scott said seriously. 'It's the only logical explanation.'

Emily opened her notebook on the flat boulder she used as a table. It was a lovely new notebook with glossy crimson covers and a gold ribbon bookmark. She flicked past her diagrams of the wreck and wrote *OPERATION COMPASS* at the top of a new page. She underlined it twice, using a new gold pen she'd bought especially for the purpose.

The familiar delicious excitement of a brand new investigation was starting to make up for the disappearance of the Pendragon compass.

Emily added the sub-heading *SUSPECTS*. 'Someone must have dived down to the wreck between the time that we left yesterday morning and first thing today when Joe and Kelly took the tour group down,' she stated.

'And it's got to be a trained scuba diver,' Scott added. 'That should narrow things down a bit.'

Emily nodded. 'A pretty experienced scuba diver, too. They must either have dived yesterday afternoon in those dangerous currents, or before it was even properly light this morning.'

Jack looked up from inspecting his sandwich. In their haste to flee The Lighthouse they'd grabbed anything they could find in the cupboards. He took a bite. Not bad! Salami, ketchup and Nutella worked surprisingly well together. 'Yeah, but who even knew the Pendragon compass was down there waiting to be nicked?' he put in.

'Exactly,' Scott said, grimacing at a tuna and banana baguette.

'Joe Gordon knew,' Emily said, writing his name at the top of the suspects list.

Jack laughed. 'But Joe was being paid to find the compass. Why would *he* steal it?'

'It's obvious!' Emily said. 'So he could sneak off and find the smugglers' hiding place and keep all the treasure for himself. Joe could have planted the toy compass there, so everyone would think that Scott was just messing about.'

'If Joe did it, he must be a world-class actor!' Scott said. He could still see Joe Gordon's face contorted with anger and disappointment – like a teacher who had just found one of his brainiest pupils skipping school to hang out at the shopping mall. To dispel the image he looked out through an arrow slit in the thick stone wall. You could see the whole bay from up here, all the way to Pirate Cove. He even thought he could make out a dark shadow where the *Mermaid* lay, but it might just have been the rocks below the waves.

'It could have been Kelly, I suppose,' Emily mused, adding the camerawoman's name to the list.

Jack was starting to enjoy this investigation now that it was firmly on dry land. 'Whoever pinched the compass will have the map to the smugglers' hoard. We've got to stop them getting their hands on all the treasure before we do.'

'We wouldn't get to *keep* the treasure,' Emily explained. 'It belongs to the company that now owns the Pendragon Estate. But I really wanted us to be the ones to find the secret location after all these years. It'd be so maddening if someone else beats us to it.'

Scott sank down onto a pile of stones cushioned with long springy grass. 'I just want to find the compass to prove to Joe Gordon I wasn't making it up. I can't bear him thinking I've been playing some pathetic prank. I mean, do I *look* like the kind of person who goes around putting Scooby-Doo compasses round skeletons' necks for laughs?'

'Joe Gordon has questioned your honour!' Jack declared in a theatrical voice. 'How dare he besmirch the illustrious name of Carter?' He leaped up and stood posing as if *en garde* for a sword fight. 'We are the Smuggling Carters of Cornwall and we will challenge the scurvy knave to a duel!'

'Will you stop banging on about the smuggling Carters?' Scott grumbled. 'We're Londoners. We're more likely to be descended from the street-sweeping Carters

of Walthamstow or the pie-selling Carters of Brixton.'
But he couldn't help laughing as Jack swashbuckled his
way around the tower. Jack's clowning around could be
dead annoying at times, but right now it was cheering
him up. He suddenly remembered how Jack had stuck
up for him against Joe as well. Yeah, Jack wasn't a bad
brother really. Scott joined in the duel, allowing Jack to
corner him against a crumbling stone pillar, with the tip
of his imaginary sword tickling Scott's ribs.

Emily sighed. This was what passed for normal
behaviour with Jack but she could usually rely on Scott
to focus on an investigation for more than five seconds.
This was like working with a pair of hyperactive goldfish
on a sugar rush! Drift wasn't helping matters by yelping
excitedly and bouncing round the boys' legs.

She studied her notebook again. So far there were
only two names on the suspects list: Joe and Kelly.
And Emily really couldn't see either of them as the
compass stealer. She supposed one of the American
group could have taken it right at the start of the tour.
She wasn't sure how they'd have known it was there,
but she added *Americans* to her list, just to make it look
a bit longer. *Now, who else could have known about
the compass?* she wondered. She hadn't told a soul
about it.

Jack leaped backwards, knocking the notebook out
of her hand.

'*Ceasefire!*' Emily yelled at the top of her voice.

Scott, Jack and Drift all stopped playing and spun round.

Emily tapped her pen on her notebook. 'We've got an investigation to run here, you know. Did either of you tell anyone else about the Pendragon compass? Scott, did you mention it to Theo Jarvis when you were hiring your equipment?'

Scott thought for a moment. 'No. I'm sure I didn't. I told him we were diving to the wreck of the *Mermaid*, but nothing else. I was too busy trying on wetsuits.'

'What about you, Jack?' Emily asked.

'Nope,' Jack said. 'Didn't breathe a word.' Then he hesitated. 'Well, actually, I suppose I might have mentioned it to Mrs White when I was at the farm. She asked me what you two were up to.'

Emily added the name *Diana White* to her list.

'You're joking,' Jack laughed. 'Mrs White's an old lady. She walks with a stick. She can't scuba dive! She said if God had meant us to swim underwater he'd have given us gills.'

Emily shook her head. 'That could all be an elaborate cover story. Did you tell anyone else?' she demanded.

'No, of course not!' Jack retorted. Then he remembered something. 'Well, apart from Aunt Kate when I was helping with the washing up last night.' He glanced at Emily. Her pen was hovering over her notebook. 'You're not *seriously* going to put Aunt Kate on your list, are you?' Jack could barely speak for

66

laughing. Aunt Kate wrote soppy romantic novels for a living and was even older than Mrs White. 'What? You think Aunt Kate has a secret past as a police frogman or a submarine captain?'

Emily smiled. 'OK. I'll leave Aunt Kate off the list.' She paused for a beat. 'For now!'

'Is there anyone else you told?' Scott asked Jack. 'Are you sure you didn't take out a full-page advert in *The Carrickstowe Times*?'

Jack stuck out his tongue at his brother.

Emily read out her list of suspects. 'Joe Gordon, Kelly Mann, Americans, Mrs White. That's all we've got.'

'Apart from *this*!' Jack pulled the Scooby-Doo compass from his pocket.

Scott clapped his hands over his eyes. 'I never want to see that stupid thing again!'

Emily took the compass and placed it inside one of the little plastic evidence bags she kept in her satchel. There was no point in looking for fingerprints on the compass, of course, as it had been found underwater. In fact, she realized, a shipwreck made a hopeless crime scene: no fingerprints, no footprints, no witnesses, no CCTV . . .

Which all added up to the *perfect* crime scene – if you were the criminal!

Eight

Emily and Jack Investigate

Before the friends left the tower they drew up a plan of action.

'Jack, you go and talk to Mrs White,' Emily instructed. 'To rule her out we need to be *sure* she can't scuba dive.'

'Aye aye, Cap'n!' Jack snapped his heels together and saluted. Another visit to Roshendra Farm would be fun. With any luck, there might even be another batch of fudge on the go.

Emily checked her watch. 'You'll find Mrs White in the library. She used to work there before she retired and she still goes back for lunch with her old colleagues on the third Wednesday of every month.'

When Jack had first met Emily he'd been amazed at how she knew the precise movements of every inhabitant on the island. Now he was used to it, but his heart sank. Libraries reminded him of school, and school reminded him of work. And what were the chances of getting his hands on some mouth-watering home-made confectionery in a *library*? But suddenly he brightened. While he was in the library he could read up about the smuggling Carters. He might even be able to trace his family tree and *prove* they were related.

'I'll go and see Theo Jarvis at the Castle Key Cabin,' Scott volunteered. 'Check whether anyone has hired out any scuba diving gear since yesterday.'

'Good idea,' Emily agreed. 'I'll go down to the harbour and have a chat with Old Bob to see if he noticed anyone unusual taking a boat out to Pirate Cove yesterday afternoon. And I'll call the tour company in Carrickstowe and see if I can track down those American tourists.' Emily's voice trailed off and she stared at Scott. 'Er, what are you eating?'

Scott looked down at the pot in his hands. 'Yoghurt. I found it in your fridge. It was the last one.' He popped a big spoonful into his mouth.

It was without doubt the most disgusting thing he'd ever tasted.

He spat it out and dropped the pot.

Emily doubled over with laughter. 'That's not yoghurt,' she spluttered. 'It's fresh yeast. Mum was going to make some bread.'

A seagull swooped down from high in the tower and pounced on the yeast. Then it spewed it out and wiped its beak on the grass.

Jack laughed. 'Maybe I was right, Scotto. You're seeing things! If you can't tell yeast from yoghurt, how can we expect you to tell Scooby-Doo from Thomas Pendragon?'

At that moment it was only the memory of the shark's jaws that prevented Scott punching Jack on the nose.

—

Emily and Drift headed to the harbour to look for Old Bob. It was now mid-afternoon and many of the smaller fishing boats were unloading their catches. Orange and blue plastic crates of mackerel and pollack were piled on the quay.

Rival gangs of gulls and gannets were brawling over a slick of spilled fish guts.

Emily noticed Old Bob's boat, *Morwenna*, tied up on the pontoon at the end of the harbour and hurried to catch him before he left for a pint at the Ship and

Anchor on his way home. Old Bob was on the deck coiling ropes. As she approached, Emily heard him speaking to someone behind him in the small cabin.

'I've not seen one that size before!' Old Bob shouted over the crackle of country and western music on a poorly tuned radio.

'Ah, it's a beauty alright!' Emily recognized the voice of Ryan Trevithick.

She was about to wave to catch Old Bob's attention when Ryan's next words stopped her in her tracks.

'You think it's a compass then, Uncle Bob?'

Compass? Suddenly all Emily's investigative instincts flicked on to red alert. She scooted back and crouched behind a pile of fish crates, pulling Drift with her.

'I'm sure of it,' Old Bob replied.

'I found it out by Pirate Cove this morning,' Ryan went on.

Emily thought she might explode with excitement. Of course! Ryan had skippered the boat to the wreck for both of the dives. He must have heard them talking about the compass and decided to have a look for himself! She could kick herself for not including him on the suspect list. But she had him in her sights now. She couldn't wait to tell the boys she'd solved the case already. Now all she had to do was get hold of that compass and they'd have directions to the smugglers' hoard.

She stepped out from behind the fish crates and strolled over to *Morwenna*.

'Ah, young Emily,' Old Bob called. 'What can we do for you?'

'Oh, I was just taking Drift for a walk,' Emily said. 'I couldn't help overhearing that you'd found a compass.'

Ryan popped his head out of the cabin. 'That's right. Great big one!'

'I'm quite interested in compasses actually,' Emily said casually. 'I could, er, take it and get it valued for you . . . save you some time?'

Ryan and Old Bob stared up at her from under matching bushy eyebrows and woollen caps.

'Valued?' Ryan laughed. 'It's not worth anything. I'll just throw it back.'

'No, don't do that!' In her alarm, Emily's voice came out as a squeak. 'I mean,' she added at a more normal pitch, 'could I at least see it first?'

Ryan shrugged. 'Sure.' He vaulted across from *Morwenna* to *Island Mist*, which was moored alongside, grabbed a boathook and poked around in a bucket sitting on the deck. Within seconds he was back, swinging the boathook in Emily's direction.

Emily shrank back as the long pole lunged towards her. Dangling from the end was a huge slimy jellyfish.

'Uggh! What's that?' Emily gulped.

'Thought you'd recognize it as you're so interested in them,' Old Bob laughed. 'It's a compass jellyfish. You can see how they got their name, with those markings like the lines on an old-fashioned compass. They don't usually venture into shallow waters.'

'It got caught up in my fishing net,' Ryan explained.

Emily tucked her hair behind her ears and leaned over, pretending to inspect the quivering mass of gloop and tentacle. 'Oh, yes, I can see now.' She glanced at her watch. 'Thanks for showing me. Lovely specimen!' she gabbled. 'Come on, Drift, we've got to get back for . . . er . . . that, you know, thing.'

Emily scuttled away along the harbour, so embarrassed that she forgot all about questioning Old Bob.

Maybe she wouldn't tell the boys about this particular phase of the investigation.

—

Meanwhile, Jack was outside the staff room of the Castle Key library where Mrs White was eating a salad lunch with the current librarian and her assistant.

Aha! Mrs White, in the library! Jack thought, peeping around the half-open door. *All we need now is Professor Plum to walk in with the lead piping and we've got a game of Cluedo on our hands!* So far, so good. But finding Mrs White was one thing. Asking her whether she had a secret scuba-diving habit was a different matter entirely. It wasn't exactly the kind of thing that cropped up in casual conversation.

Jack racked his brains for an opening line. *So, Mrs White, I'm afraid the ex-librarian-farmer's-wife-with-*

a-walking-stick disguise doesn't work on me. Admit it, you're secretly a highly trained frogman on special ops! No, maybe not. Jack peeped round the door again. Mrs White was packing her lunch things away, feeling around next to her chair for her stick. *I've got to come up with something fast before they see me lurking here and throw me out for defacing books or something.* If Emily were here, no doubt she'd have some cunning plan, and Scott would just schmooze his way in being all charming and polite.

Suddenly, Jack had a flash of pure genius.

He knocked on the door. 'Excuse me, does anyone know where I can find a book on scuba diving?' He smiled at the three ladies so sweetly he almost made himself sick. 'My brother was diving yesterday and he thinks he might have caught nitro-septic diving fever from his oxygen tank.'

Mrs White shook her head sympathetically. 'Oh, dear, that does sound nasty.'

Jack grinned. Mrs White was definitely in the clear. Anyone who'd done five minutes of a diving course would know he'd been talking total rubbish. You don't have pure oxygen in a scuba tank. And as for nitro-septic diving fever, Jack had just made it up.

'Try the sports section,' the assistant librarian suggested.

'I'll help you look,' Mrs White offered.

Jack pretended to consult the scuba diving guide

75

that Mrs White pulled off the shelf for him. 'Looks like Scott'll live,' he said, clapping the book shut. 'I *told* him that nasty rash was probably just advanced acne.'

Mrs White smiled. 'Poor boy. I'm glad it's nothing serious.'

Sorted, Jack thought. *Now, let's check out these Smuggling Carters.* He was about to head off to the local history section when he had another brainwave. He was really on a roll today! If he asked nicely, perhaps he could get Mrs White to do the legwork for him . . .

Ten minutes later, Jack was idly rocking on the back legs of his chair while Mrs White was working through a pile of dusty history books, parish records and old newspapers.

'It looks as if someone else has had these records out recently,' she murmured. 'They're all out of order.' After some time, she took off her reading glasses. 'Your father's Leo Carter, isn't he? And is his father called William Carter?'

Jack nodded.

Mrs White smiled. 'Perfect. Now, I've drawn it all out here for you.'

Jack looked down at the diagram. It looked like a food web in a science book, except much more complicated. And it had his name at the bottom, where the plankton should be.

'It's your family tree,' Mrs White told him. 'I've gone right back to the eighteenth century.'

Jack was so excited he lost his balance. The back legs of the chair shot forward, screeching over the tiles, and the next thing he knew he was spread-eagled on the floor.

Everyone in the library looked round.

'Nothing to see here!' Jack mumbled, picking himself up and righting the chair.

He sat back down and turned to Mrs White. 'Am I . . .' he stammered. 'Am I *really* a Smuggling Carter?'

Nine

Interesting Reading

Mrs White beamed at Jack. 'You are indeed a descendant of the famous Carter family. In fact, you're the great-great-and-a-few-more-greats grandson of John Carter himself. He was the head of the family. He was known as the King of Prussia and ran one of the biggest smuggling operations in Cornwall. The place the family lived is still called Prussia Cove. It's on the mainland near Penzance.' She traced her finger over the family tree. 'We know a lot about the Carters because one of the brothers, Harry, wrote *An Autobiography of a Cornish Smuggler*. There's a book about them you can take home to read if you like.'

Jack grinned. He couldn't wait to tell Scott he'd been right all along. They had Cornish smuggling blood in their veins! And when he got back to London, he'd have major bragging rights! He bet his friends Josh and Ali didn't have such cool ancestors. He might even work it up a bit to include a few pirates and a highwayman too...

He glanced at the open books on the desk. They were full of stories about sea battles with the revenue men, galloping over moonlit cliffs on horseback, false-bottomed barrels filled with rum. Maybe he'd have to read some of this stuff. He noticed some of the other names Mrs White had jotted down along with the Carters: Black Joan, Mad George Mann, Cruel Copinger, Battling Bill and, of course, Thomas Pendragon. They sounded like a wild bunch.

But as he thanked Mrs White and left the library, Jack had the peculiar sensation that Thomas Pendragon wasn't the *only* name on that list that sounded familiar...

⌣

Bursting with his news, Jack raced back to The Lighthouse, where he'd arranged to meet Scott and

Emily at three (or, to use Emily's words, *to rendezvous for a Situation Report at fifteen hundred hours*). He was the first back to base. Emily's mum called down the spiral staircase from the kitchen to say she was up to her elbows in bread dough (*She must have found some more yeast*, Jack thought, laughing at the memory of Scott's face). Mrs Wild told him to help himself to a Coke from the sideboard and to make himself at home until the others got back.

Jack *always* felt at home in The Lighthouse! It was one of his favourite places in the world. The big circular guest lounge on the ground floor was bright and cosy with its colourful rugs and wall hangings.

Jack grabbed a drink and sprawled on one of the squashy sofas. There was nobody else around, so he put his feet up on the coffee table and began reading the library book. Soon he was immersed in a brilliantly gory story. His ancestor, Harry Carter, was horribly injured in a battle with the customs men and left for dead, but he'd managed to crawl to shore. His nose was hanging on by a shred of skin, and there were bits of his skull coming out of his head . . .

Cool! Jack thought. *Gross, but cool!* Unable to stop reading, he put his Coke down on the coffee table without looking up. The can toppled over. He caught it and started mopping up with the hem of his t-shirt. A few splashes of Coke had landed on some books and notes that had been left scattered all over the coffee table.

As he dabbed, he couldn't help noticing familiar words: *customs, contraband, Cornwall*. Hang on, this was like *Groundhog Day*! He'd seen all this stuff in the library. He forgot about the Coke, picked up a photocopied page and began to read . . .

When the smuggling vessel the Mermaid ran aground in Pirate Cove, it was thought that all hands were lost, but one of Thomas Pendragon's men survived. He was found guilty of smuggling and sentenced to be hanged from the gibbet on Castle Key common. However, due to a public outcry, the death sentence was reduced and he was transported to the colonies.

Jack made himself comfortable on the sofa again and kept reading.

As he boarded the convict ship for Australia, George Mann swore vengeance on the informant who had betrayed Pendragon to the revenue men.

The words *Australia, George Mann* and *vengeance* had been underlined with yellow highlighter.

Jack's brain went into overdrive.

Slowly, he reached for an envelope that had been tucked inside a pile of notes as a bookmark. He turned it over.

It was addressed to *Miss K. Mann.*

These notes belonged to Kelly!

Of course! The familiar name he'd seen in Mrs White's notes in the library was *Mann*! Suddenly the pieces of the puzzle were falling into place. George Mann had been deported to Australia. Kelly Mann was *from* Australia. She was obviously one of his descendants.

Jack studied the photocopied page again. Kelly had jotted some notes in the margin: *Who betrayed Pendragon's men??? (1) Find name of informant (2) Track down descendants still in this area.*

He picked up another page to find more notes: *Proud Cornish family. Honour at stake. Long memories? Revenge!*

Revenge was underlined!

Jack snatched his hand back as if he'd received an electric shock. He could hardly believe his eyes – but the evidence was staring him in the face. It seemed that being a camerawoman for Joe Gordon's project was just a cover story. The *real* reason Kelly had come to Castle Key was to get revenge on the family of the informer who'd betrayed her ancestor all those centuries ago.

Jack read another of Kelly's notes: *Check who owns any remaining smuggled goods. Family?* Another massive puzzle piece zoomed into place. Kelly was trying to find the smugglers' hoard!

She obviously believed the treasure was her family inheritance.

And then it hit him. *Kelly must be the one who stole the Pendragon compass from the wreck!*

It all made perfect sense!

At that moment, Jack heard footsteps outside the front door. Oh no, Kelly was coming back! She must have only popped out for some fresh air or something. If she caught him snooping through her notes he was going to be in major trouble. With his pulse racing he scanned the pages on the table. He desperately needed just one more piece of information: *who was the informant whose family Kelly Mann had come to hunt down and punish?*

Jack glanced up to see the door handle turning.

He took one last look at the notes. *He just needed a name.*

And then he saw it!

Enraged by a dispute over a missing silver candlestick at Pendragon Manor, a chambermaid called Annie Cuttance tipped off the revenue men that the Mermaid would be coming ashore in Pirate Cove that night, laden with contraband.

Annie Cuttance was underlined.

Yes! He had a name.

Jack was about to leap away from the coffee table

when he caught a glimpse of something that snapped him back like industrial-strength elastic.

Scribbled in the margin were the words, *Informant's family? Irene Cuttance. Married Norman Loveday, 1962.*

And below that, circled in thick red marker pen: *FIND MRS L.*

Ten

Revenge is Sweet

Emily pushed open the front door of The Lighthouse to see Jack standing next to the coffee table holding a piece of paper. She was about to say hello when he dropped the paper, sprang three feet high in a vertical take-off and landed on the other side of the guest lounge, where he leaned against the wall pretending to admire a painting of a vase of poppies. The last time Emily had seen anyone look so guilty was when she'd caught Drift with his nose in her mum's shopping bag and buttercream icing all over his face.

'What are you doing?' she asked.

Jack clutched his chest in relief. 'I thought you were . . .' he gasped. 'Never mind . . . I've just seen . . . You won't believe . . . betrayal . . . Australia . . . revenge . . . Mrs Loveday . . .'

Emily stared. Jack stood opening and closing his mouth, pointing at the coffee table with one hand and making throat-cutting gestures with the other. Had he flipped his lid? She tried to remember what she'd read in her *Survival Guide for Secret Agents* about how to deal with freak-outs and funny turns. *Speak calmly and quietly . . .* Cautiously, Emily approached the coffee table to investigate. Was it a spider? She knew how Jack felt about spiders . . .

Next moment, Jack was rugby-tackling her away from the table as if she'd been about to step on a live grenade.

'She might come back . . .' he spluttered.

Emily gave up on the *calmly-and-quietly* approach. She gripped Jack firmly by the elbow and marched him towards the spiral staircase. Maybe she could get some sense out of him if they got away from the coffee table.

Jack collapsed onto a beanbag in Emily's room on the eighth floor. After several false starts he finally got the story out.

At first Emily didn't believe it. 'It's true that Mrs Loveday's surname was Cuttance before she got married. But do you really think Kelly's got some sort of vendetta against her because of something that happened hundreds of years ago? Are you sure that's not just wishful thinking? I know Mrs Loveday's not exactly your favourite person.'

'Think about it!' Jack said. 'Mrs Loveday is the biggest nosey-parker on the planet, right? Remember when we were investigating the hidden gold on Gulliver's Island? It turned out to be Mrs Loveday's granny who'd told tales about the lighthouse keeper. Being a busybody obviously runs in the family. No wonder Annie Cuttance shopped Thomas Pendragon to the customs men just because he'd found her nicking the silver or something.'

Emily still wasn't convinced. But then she crept downstairs and saw it with her own eyes: Kelly Mann's notes traced the family tree from the woman who betrayed Pendragon through to Mrs Irene Loveday – whose maiden name was Cuttance. And just as Jack said, there was that chilling word – *Revenge!* – and then, circled in red, *FIND MRS L.*

It seemed Operation Compass had just changed direction!

Emily took a photo of the evidence on her phone and sprinted back up the one hundred and twenty steps to her room, stopping only to listen outside Guest Room Two on the third floor. She could hear Kelly moving around inside. It sounded as if she were getting ready to go out.

Back in her room, Emily stuffed her full investigation kit into her satchel.

'What do you think Kelly will do when she finds Mrs Loveday?' Jack asked.

'I don't know. But if she's come all the way from Australia she must mean business. We have to find Mrs Loveday before Kelly does – and warn her.'

Jack began wrestling his way out of the beanbag. He was pinned down by Drift, who'd climbed in for a snooze on his lap. He also began wrestling with his conscience. Being descended from a proud old Cornish smuggling family himself, he could identify with Kelly Mann. If she wanted to avenge her family's honour, good for her! And, as for Mrs Loveday, she'd taken an instant dislike to Jack from their first meeting last summer and had treated him like something she'd found on the bottom of her shoe ever since. He'd quite like to see her get a taste of her own medicine! *And yet*, his conscience piped up – in that annoying way it always did just when he didn't want to listen – *what if Kelly's planning something really drastic like stealing all Mrs Loveday's savings or burning her house down?*

Jack decided Emily was right – they had to warn Mrs Loveday.

Emily was already on her way out of the door. 'Come on, you two!' she told Jack and Drift. 'Mrs Loveday will be at Dotty's Tea Rooms now. She always goes there on Wednesday afternoons after she finishes her cleaning job at the vicarage.'

'Aren't we going to wait for Scott?' Jack asked.

Emily sighed impatiently. 'We can't hang about. Kelly could be about to murder Mrs Loveday in cold blood!'

In the middle of Dotty's Tea Rooms? Jack thought. *What's she going to do? Gun her down with a sawn-off teacake?*

—

Jack, Emily and Drift crouched outside the window of Dotty's Tea Rooms and peeped in.

Mrs Loveday was sitting at a table near the window with a cup of tea. Sporting her usual attire of pink cycle helmet, orange high-visibility vest, flowery dress and checked apron, the old lady was pretending to be engrossed in a sudoku puzzle in a magazine – although she was clearly earwigging on Dotty's conversation with Laura Roberts at the counter.

Emily breathed a sigh of relief. They'd made it in time to warn her about Kelly. She looked both ways to check the coast was clear and was about to head for the door when Jack grabbed her t-shirt and pulled her into the alley that ran between Dotty's and the Castle Key Cabin. Drift tucked in behind them.

'What?' Emily hissed, but Jack held up a finger to silence her. Then she saw why. A short, plump figure in cropped jeans and a voluminous black t-shirt was hurrying along the seafront.

It was Kelly Mann!

She must have left The Lighthouse right behind us, Emily realized. *And she's coming this way!*

Emily and Jack exchanged looks of wide-eyed dismay as Kelly Mann walked right past them and entered the café.

The friends quickly crept back to the window and watched as Kelly hurried to Mrs Loveday's table and sat down. Kelly was smiling and shaking her head and pointing to her watch as if apologizing for being late.

Cool customer! Emily thought. You'd think she was meeting an old friend for a coffee, not hunting down her family's sworn enemy.

Kelly pulled out a notebook.

Emily rummaged in her investigation kit and pulled out a listening device she'd made using a set of headphones and the little amplifiers from an old hearing aid. She'd tried it out at home and she'd been dying for a chance to use it for real. She pressed the amplifier to the window and put on the headphones. There was some crackling and rustling, and then Kelly's strident voice.

'So, am I getting this down right, Irene? Your maiden name was Cuttance and your father was called John?'

Emily gasped. Jack was right! Kelly was quizzing Mrs Loveday all about her family tree. She was obviously making sure she'd got the right person before wreaking some terrible vengeance.

Jack saw Emily's face and couldn't bear the suspense a moment longer. He snatched the headphones and pulled them on. His mouth dropped open at Kelly's next words . . .

'Are you the last of the Cuttance line, Irene? Or are there other family members living locally?'

This was even bigger than he'd thought! Kelly Mann wasn't just after Mrs Loveday. She was planning to wipe out the entire Cuttance clan!

'Well, no, dear,' Mrs Loveday told Kelly. 'There's my son, Kevin, of course. And my sister, Pat, in Carrickstowe, although we don't talk about her since all that to-do with the caravan in Falmouth . . .' The old lady was clearly having the time of her life regaling Kelly with all the family history and hearsay she could dredge up from her bottomless pit of gossip.

Jack held out one half of the headphones so Emily could hear too and then watched as Kelly went to the counter, spoke to Dotty for a moment and returned to the table with a plate of small iced chocolate cakes. Mrs Loveday's eyes lit up greedily as she reached for the largest one. 'Ooh, my favourites. Are you having one, dear?'

'I'd better not!' Kelly's voice boomed through the listening device. 'Got to watch the old weight!'

Jack stared at Emily in horror. He wasn't buying that hogwash about weight-watching. There was only *one* reason you'd say no to chocolate cakes that looked *that* good. Jack turned to Emily. He could tell from her face that she knew it too.

'Kelly's poisoned the cakes!' they whispered in unison.

The cake was now halfway between the plate and Mrs Loveday's mouth.

'We're going in!' Emily yelled.

Together, they burst through the café door with a mighty jangling of the bell and threw themselves at Mrs Loveday's table.

Eleven

A Lot of Explaining

While Jack and Emily were spying on Kelly Mann, Scott wasn't far away. In fact, he was next door in the Castle Key Cabin interviewing Theo Jarvis. There were no major breakthroughs in the case – Theo confirmed that he hadn't hired out scuba diving kit to anyone except Scott in the last few days – but they'd ended up having a good long chat about football and bands and computer games.

Theo is one cool guy, Scott thought, as he said goodbye and strolled back out onto the seafront.

He was about to head back to The Lighthouse when he glanced towards Dotty's Tea Rooms. He spotted three familiar figures crouching outside on the pavement with their noses pressed up against the window. He jogged over to see what was going on but, before he could reach them, Jack, Emily and Drift suddenly stormed into the café like a SWAT team on a dawn raid.

Scott hurried to follow, catching the door as it rebounded from their dramatic entrance.

He was greeted by a scene of total pandemonium.

Scott did a double take.

He couldn't believe what his eyes were telling him!

Had Jack *really* just snatched a chocolate cake right out of Mrs Loveday's hand, knocking her cup of tea flying into the air?

And was Emily *really* swiping an entire plate of chocolate cakes from under Kelly Mann's nose and sprinting across the café with them?

Now Jack and Emily were heading for the door. Neither of them was looking where they were going and they both crashed into Scott, who held out his arms to block their path.

'We've been mugged,' Mrs Loveday squawked, leaping up and dabbing tea from her lap with a napkin, 'by a gang of Teenage Hoodwinks!'

'You mean *hoodlums*?' Kelly asked, looking more bemused than frightened.

'Exactly!' Mrs Loveday patted her chest as if to check her heart was still beating. 'Mindless thugs, roaming the streets, no regard for decent Law-Dividing Citizens!' She glared down at Drift, who was under the table looking for cake crumbs. 'Letting their dangerous dogs run out of control, too!'

'Don't worry, Mrs L,' Kelly said, trying to calm the old lady. 'It's only Emily from The Lighthouse. She's a good kid. I should know. She saved my life the other day!' Kelly turned to Jack. 'And you're Scott's brother, aren't you?' Kelly looked from the chocolate cake in Jack's hand to the plate in Emily's and back again. 'So, what's the story, kids? Are you on a scavenger hunt or something?'

Before Jack and Emily could answer, Mrs Loveday was off again. 'Well, well, well,' she tutted, scowling at Jack and nodding as if she'd expected something like this all along. 'I'm afraid this doesn't surprise me. He's from *London*, you know. That's on the mainland,' she explained to Kelly as if, being foreign, she might not have heard of it. 'In *London* they'd mug an old lady for a chocolate *button*, let alone a chocolate cake.'

'I *wasn't* mugging you . . .' Jack muttered.

'We were just trying to . . .' Emily began.

But Mrs Loveday was in full spate. 'And as for you, young lady! You should know better! Carry on like this and you're headed for a life in the Criminal Underwear.'

'Criminal *underworld*,' Kelly corrected.

'Quite right, dear,' Mrs Loveday folded her arms across her chest. 'It's a slippery slope.'

Scott still had no idea what was going on but he knew he had to get Emily and Jack away before Mrs Loveday called the police and had them all carted off to a young offenders' unit. He fetched a cloth from the counter and helped mop up. Then he brought Mrs Loveday a fresh pot of tea. 'I'm so sorry,' he said, in his best Charming Young Man voice. 'You'll have to excuse my brother. He's got this unfortunate brain problem. Sometimes he can't control his actions.'

Mrs Loveday looked unconvinced. But Kelly nodded sympathetically. 'So *that's* why he couldn't come on the dive with us?' She smiled at Jack. 'Poor kid!'

'I didn't . . . I'm not . . . I haven't . . .' Jack spluttered.

Meanwhile, Emily was still standing near the door holding the plate of chocolate cakes in front of her like a waitress who's forgotten which table to go to. 'Emily's just very, er, *hungry*,' Scott said, hardly able to believe the feebleness of the cover story that was coming out of his mouth. 'Yeah, she didn't have time for breakfast or lunch, because she's been so busy helping her mum at The Lighthouse . . .'

Mrs Loveday sank into her chair and stared at Emily. 'Your parents should be ashamed of themselves. That's Child Exploration!'

Kelly shook her head. 'She's skin and bones, poor little waif!'

Any minute now, Scott thought, *Mrs Loveday will be reporting Emily's parents to social services.* 'Come on!' he urged Emily in a 'let's be sensible' voice. 'Give the cakes back. I'll buy you a pasty.' He pushed her firmly towards the table. Emily resisted, clinging on to the plate, looking round desperately with big, pleading eyes. Scott just couldn't figure it out. *If I hadn't seen her eat several tuna and banana sandwiches two hours ago, I'd really believe Emily was starving.*

Kelly smiled at Emily. 'It's OK. You keep the cakes. You obviously need them more than we do.'

Mrs Loveday didn't look very convinced by that argument but she forced a smile and nodded.

Still mumbling apologies, Scott bundled Jack, Emily and Drift out of the café.

—

As soon as they were outside, Jack grabbed the plate of cakes from Emily, jumped over the harbour wall and took off across the beach. 'Quick, let's chuck them in the sea before we're contaminated!'

'No, don't do that!' Emily yelled, racing after him with Drift at her heels. 'Those cakes are *evidence*!'

When Scott caught them up, he found Emily, wearing plastic gloves, using tweezers to transfer the cakes into an extra-large evidence bag from her satchel.

Scott looked slowly from his brother to his friend and back again. 'Could someone explain why we're now going around stealing chocolate cakes from old ladies?'

⌢

The explanations lasted all the way to The Lighthouse, where the friends flopped down on the sofas in the guest lounge.

At first Scott was doubtful. What with the combination of Jack's over-active imagination and Emily's obsession with smugglers, the two of them had clearly got totally carried away with all this nonsense about Kelly avenging her family's honour.

'Hello-oo, in case you hadn't noticed, this is the twenty-first century!' he laughed. 'The world's moved on. We've got Instant Messaging and yoghurt-in-a-tube and microwave popcorn and everything. You're not seriously saying that Kelly is trying to annihilate Mrs Loveday's family for something that happened over two hundred years ago?'

But then Emily showed him her photos of Kelly's notes, and Scott started to wonder if they might just have a point – although he still wasn't totally convinced about *all* the details.

'How could Kelly Mann have poisoned those cakes without anyone noticing?' he asked.

'Easy!' Jack insisted. 'While Dotty's back was turned at the counter she whipped out a little sachet of arsenic or something and sprinkled it on like hundreds and thousands.'

Scott had to give Jack full marks for creativity!

'Anyway,' Emily said. 'I don't think Kelly will try anything else just yet. After all that kerfuffle, she'll probably want to lie low for a bit before striking again. We need to plan our next move . . .'

'Hang on, I haven't even told Scott the best part yet,' Jack interrupted. 'I did loads of research in the library this afternoon. I've got this amazing family tree and everything. It proves that we really are related to the Smuggling Carters of Prussia Cove.'

That's when Emily looked up and saw Kelly Mann in the doorway.

Twelve

Family History

Kelly Mann smiled. 'Hi kids, I couldn't help overhearing!'

Emily gaped at her in dismay. How long had Kelly been standing there? How much had she heard? Did she know that her poisoned cake plot had been rumbled?

Kelly strode across the room and sank down next to Jack on the sofa. 'Did you just say you're related to the Carter family of Prussia Cove?'

Emily exchanged glances of relief with Scott. With luck, that was the *only* part Kelly had heard.

Jack nodded proudly, forgetting all about Kelly being their Prime Suspect. 'Arrr, that's right. We're good old Cornish smugglers and proud of it!'

Scott had to gulp back a snort of laughter. Jack was actually trying to pull off a Cornish accent. He sounded like the world's first Cockney pirate.

'Hey, good on ya!' Kelly laughed. 'Me too! I've been tracing my family history for ages. I found out my roots go back to this bloke called George Mann. He worked for Thomas Pendragon and was the only survivor when the *Mermaid* sank. He was shipped off to Oz. What a story, eh? That's why I took this filming job with Joe Gordon. He's not paying me much, but it was a chance to come to Cornwall. I got in touch with a British TV company and pitched the idea of a documentary film to them – you know, *Cornwall's Smuggling Past*, that kind of thing. I wanted to trace the descendants of the old smuggling families and see what they're doing now. The TV company is keen but they want me to really big up the "human interest" angle.'

'What do you mean?' Scott asked.

'They want heaps of drama! Like feuds still going on between families because someone's great-great-granny betrayed someone else's great-great-grandad to the customs men. I can't imagine anyone bearing a grudge from that far back, but I said I'd dig around and see what I could find.'

'So,' Emily asked slowly, 'you're just tracking people down to *interview* them?'

Kelly nodded. 'I got some great stuff today. That Mrs Loveday didn't know much about Annie Cuttance but she's a real mine of information. Sweet old lady!'

Kelly was clearly deluded if she thought Mrs Loveday was *sweet*, Emily thought. But apart from that, her story rang true. She wasn't after revenge at all, just some exciting material for her documentary film. Emily had never felt so dumb. She knew she shouldn't have listened to Jack!

Kelly slapped Jack on the back. 'So, you've been doing some research too, eh? Can I see? Hey, could I interview you for my film?'

Jack grinned and handed Kelly his notes. Finding out he was a famous Cornish smuggler *and* being offered a starring role in a film wasn't bad for a day's work!

Kelly began to study the family tree. 'Great stuff! You're a real pro at this.'

Jack squirmed with a tiny pang of guilt at taking all the credit for Mrs White's work, but it was too late to come clean now.

Scott glanced at one of the pages. That wasn't Jack's writing! It was far too neat for a start. 'You didn't do this!' he snorted. Then he remembered his deal with the shark and hastily changed to an admiring tone. 'Wow!

You didn't do this *all this afternoon*, did you? That's awesome!'

Jack eyed his brother with suspicion. Why did Scott keep being nice to him? What was he after? But he didn't spend too much time wondering. Something had just occurred to him: if Kelly Mann had been innocently interviewing Mrs Loveday and not trying to bump her off with toxic sprinkles, then that meant . . .

He glanced down at Emily's bag on the floor next to her chair. Surely it would be a shame to let six perfectly good chocolate cakes go to waste. A crime, even! And he *was* feeling a bit peckish. Those Nutella and salami sandwiches at lunchtime hadn't been very filling. Maybe he'd just have one little nibble. Quietly, he reached into the evidence bag and helped himself.

Kelly had been studying Jack's notes for some time when she suddenly looked up and slapped her forehead. 'I just remembered something I wanted to show you guys.' She hurried up to her room and returned with her video camera. It looked small and fragile stripped of its lights and waterproof housing, like a snail without its shell. 'Last night I was looking through all my footage of the wreck. I think I caught a shot of something inside the deck on that first dive, just before I got all tangled up in that fishing line.'

She handed the camera to Scott.

Excitement flickered under Scott's ribs. *What sort of something?* He peered at the small playback screen. Through the dark water, the camera lights had picked out smudges of white. Scott recognized them straight away. 'That's the skeleton I saw!' he exclaimed. 'This must be before it fell down along with that plank that trapped Emily's foot. It's still quite high up above the gap here.'

'That's right,' Kelly agreed. 'I didn't even notice it at the time. I was so busy trying to free myself. That's why the film is out of focus. And then I dropped the camera, of course.'

Scott was already pressing the button to play the film again. *If the camera captured the skeleton, maybe it caught the compass too.* He froze the frame where the skeleton came into view. He could just about make out a round blob in front of the skull. He zoomed in. Yes, that was it! The compass was dangling down past the skeleton's nose, just as he remembered it. 'Has Joe seen this?' he asked.

'Not yet,' Kelly said. 'He had to go up to Bristol yesterday for some meetings. He'll be back in a couple of days. But I can email him this image.'

Scott thanked her. 'Then perhaps he'll believe I really *did* see the Pendragon compass and I'm not just some pathetic prankster!'

Kelly smiled. 'Yeah. Joe's a great bloke, really. I'm

sorry he was so hard on you. It was just that he was so stoked to think you'd found the compass. He was as mad as a cut snake when it disappeared.'

Suddenly Scott had an idea. 'Can you output this onto your laptop? We should be able to enhance the image and get more detail.'

'No worries,' Kelly said, clearly impressed by Scott's technical know-how.

While Kelly and Scott worked on the film, Emily took out her notebook. She was delighted that Scott had been proved right, of course, but it didn't solve the question of who had stolen the compass from the skeleton's neck and left the Scooby-Doo toy in its place. And how could they track down the smuggler's secret hoard without it? She discreetly crossed Kelly Mann off the suspect list. 'What about Mrs White?' she asked Jack. 'Did you find anything out?'

Jack recalled Mrs White's response to his nitro-septic diving fever fib. 'Definitely innocent,' he replied. Except – due to the large quantity of chocolate cake in his mouth – it came out as *meffaly immofup*.

Emily's eyes followed the trail of cake crumbs down the front of Jack's t-shirt, across the sofa to the empty evidence bag in her satchel.

Jack grinned sheepishly. 'Tasty bit of evidence, that!'

'Look!' Scott cried, beckoning them to the laptop screen. 'You can see it much better now.'

Emily and Jack leaned in to study the image. It was

still blurry but they could make out a roughly octagonal object. It was coated in a shell of sandy concretion, but a fragment of the casing had broken away at one edge to reveal faint lines engraved into the brass lid of the compass underneath.

Emily snapped shut her notebook. Maybe they didn't need the compass to find the smugglers' hiding place after all. Perhaps the map was right in front of their eyes!

Scott zoomed in to enlarge the image of the exposed section of the compass.

Emily stared. Then she closed her eyes and groaned with disappointment. The lines she'd seen weren't part of a map at all. They wove in and out of each other in a complicated Celtic knot pattern. It was just a useless decorative border!

Jack was unimpressed too. 'All this fuss over a rusty old compass with a stupid squiggly pattern round the edge. It probably doesn't even work any more with that concrete gunk, or whatever it's called, all over it!'

Scott rolled his eyes. 'I don't think you'll be getting a job on *Antiques Roadshow* any time soon.'

First thing next morning, Emily went looking for Old Bob to ask whether any unusual boats had been seen heading for Pirate Cove in the critical period between the first dive when Scott had seen Pendragon's compass around the skeleton's neck, and the second one when Joe Gordon found that it had been replaced by the Scooby-Doo toy. She found the old fisherman tuning *Morwenna*'s engine, and this time there were no jellyfish lurking in buckets of seawater. Old Bob was used to Emily's odd questions. He thought for a moment, rubbing a gnarly hand over his old woollen cap, but then he shook his head. 'No. I've not noticed anything out of the ordinary these last few days.'

Emily thanked him and walked away. Drift trotted along behind her, happily sniffing out the tiny crabs that scuttled under the heaps of washed up seaweed. Emily, on the other hand, couldn't help feeling dejected as she mooched along the pebbly beach. It seemed the Pendragon compass had vanished into thin air – or thin water, to be precise. No boats had been seen going out to Pirate Cove, nobody had hired diving equipment from the Castle Key Cabin, and the suspect list was getting shorter by the minute: Mrs White couldn't scuba dive, Kelly Mann was only interested in getting good stories for her documentary film, and Emily's phone call to the tour company had revealed that the entire group of American tourists had boarded a coach to London immediately after they'd returned from the wreck dive. If one of them had taken the compass, there wasn't much she could do about it.

That left Joe Gordon. Could Joe have switched the

compasses so he could search for the smugglers' hoard for himself? Emily wasn't convinced, but she'd have to interview him on his return from Bristol. It was starting to look like the only possible explanation.

But just then, she looked up to see a truck reversing down the ramp at the end of the harbour. It was towing a trailer with a small rowing boat on board. Emily suddenly had a brainwave.

Old Bob hadn't seen any boats heading out to Pirate Cove. But there was one other way the compass-stealer could have got to the wreck.

Maybe Joe Gordon wasn't the only explanation after all!

Emily pulled out her phone and called the boys. 'Meet me at the castle,' she told them. 'We're going for a walk.'

Thirteen

Drift Finds a Clue

'A walk?' Jack grumbled, as he and Scott joined Emily in the tower. 'What for?' Jack didn't really *get* walks. You went somewhere, turned around and came back. What was the point?

Emily ignored him and held out a map she'd sketched in her notebook while waiting. 'There's an old track,' she said. 'It runs from here down to Pirate Cove.'

Jack nodded. He remembered how their friends Max Fordham and Savannah Shaw had escaped down that track last summer, just after Jack had rescued Savannah from the cliff edge – an act of supreme heroic awesomeness, though he said so himself. 'What's that got to do with the compass?' he asked

'What if the compass thief *drove* to Pirate Cove?' Emily's words tumbled over each other with excitement. 'It's steep and bumpy, but if you've got a jeep with four-wheel drive, you can get almost as far as the beach. You could easily take a small kayak on the roof, so you could paddle out into the cove and dive to the *Mermaid*.' She looked triumphantly from Jack to Scott as if daring them to disagree.

Scott grinned. 'Let me guess. This *walk* you mentioned, it wouldn't involve the track to Pirate Cove and searching for clues, would it?'

Emily was already on her way out of the tower. 'How did you guess?'

'It's an old smuggling path,' Emily explained as the three friends and Drift trekked down the steep hill. 'Sometimes the smugglers would hide the contraband down in the rocks and then the farmers would come at night to fetch it. They'd load all the stuff onto their mules and lead them up this way. That's why the sides are banked up so steeply. So the revenue men couldn't see their lights.'

Jack looked around. The lane was like a green tunnel,

with high banks and blossom-loaded hedges that met overhead. Butterflies flitted among the foxgloves and cowslips that smothered the banks. But in Jack's mind it was a stormy night, the wind was howling and blowing clouds across the moon, and he was hurrying down the path to retrieve barrels of brandy from the beach. He could almost hear the clopping of the mules' hooves behind him.

When the lane had dropped down almost to the shore it flattened out to a small patch of sandy grass.

'You'd have to park and walk over the rocks to the beach from here,' Emily explained.

'Brilliant,' Jack said. 'Let's look for footprints in the sand.'

Emily shook her head. 'The tide will have washed them away.'

Scott pointed to a patch of grass and foxgloves with bent and broken stems. 'This could be where the vehicle parked.'

'Let's look for tyre prints,' Jack suggested.

Emily shook her head again. 'Sorry, the wind will have blown sand over them by now.'

Jack sighed. 'So you're saying that the sum total of this mammoth Clue Fest is a few broken stalks?'

Emily pulled three magnifying glasses from her bag. 'No. I'm saying we should do a fingertip search of the entire area. The thief is bound to have dropped *something*.'

But half an hour later, Scott, Emily and Jack had nothing to show for their search – except for sore knees and stiff backs.

Jack had had enough. He dropped to his knees. 'One little tiny clue!' he bellowed at no one in particular, brandishing his magnifying glass. 'A sweet wrapper. A cigarette end. Is it too much to ask?'

Scott shrugged. 'Looks like it.'

'Hey!' Emily cried. 'Drift's found something!'

Drift was sniffing in the scrubby grass near the broken foxgloves. He looked up, his ears standing to attention, and barked once.

Jack rushed to see what Drift had found.

To his surprise the object between Drift's paws looked like a rough sandy pebble.

Jack picked it up and turned it over in his hand. It was the size of his palm, but less heavy than a stone. In fact, it was hollow, more like a clamshell. 'False alarm! It's just a shell!' he told the others. 'Not exactly a show-stopping clue, when you're right next to a beach!'

Emily knelt down and stroked Drift's ears. 'There must be something special about it,' she said. 'Drift doesn't normally bark at shells.'

Drift flicked his ear – the white one with brown spots – in agreement.

Jack nudged the ground with his toe. 'There's another one the same here. Looks like it's the other half.' He picked it up and handed it to Emily.

Emily was puzzled. The outside was rough and grainy. The inside was much smoother, but when she ran her fingers over it, she could feel grooves and ridges. She took out her magnifying glass for a closer look. Suddenly, she knew they were on to something big. *This wasn't a shell.* She was so excited she could hardly speak. In the end she only managed a single word.

'Concretion!' she gasped.

'What?' said Jack.

But Scott knew in an instant. Of course! Emily was right. Last time he'd seen this 'shell' it had been hanging from the neck of a skeleton. He could even see the eight sides now he looked properly. And there was a piece missing on one side just as they'd seen on Kelly's video. 'This is the crust that encased the Pendragon compass! Well done, Drift. This has cracked the case wide open – literally.'

'What are you talking about?' Jack asked.

'The thief must have come back here to his vehicle after nicking the compass from the wreck,' Emily explained. 'He – or she – couldn't wait to have a look, so they sat here and chipped off the casing. They just left the pieces lying on the ground before driving off.'

'It would've been handy if they'd dropped the compass as well,' Jack grumbled. 'This concrete stuff isn't going to help us find the smugglers' hoard.'

'That's just where you're wrong!' Emily said. She held the casing out to him. 'Feel that.'

'Er, yeah. It's all rough. Like an old brick or something.'

'Not that side, you dingbat,' Scott snorted. Then he remembered the shark. 'Yeah, easy mistake to make, but try the inside.'

Jack ran his fingers over the inside of the casing as if he were reading Braille. 'I can just feel some bumpy bits . . .'

'Exactly!' Emily said. 'I think those lines are prints of whatever was engraved on the base and the lid of the compass.'

Jack gazed down at the crusty shells with new-found respect. 'Wow! You mean the clues to the secret hoard could be on here?'

Scott nodded. 'We just need to take some kind of impression so we can see them.'

Jack headed back to the path. 'What are we waiting for? Let's go and get some soap.'

'Soap?' Scott and Emily echoed.

'To make an impression, of course!' Jack said. 'I saw it in a film. They copied a key.'

'That's only when people are stuck in prison or something and they can't get hold of anything else,' Scott explained.

'I've got a better idea,' Emily said, overtaking Jack and running up the steep track with Drift. 'Let's get back to The Lighthouse.'

Fourteen

The Secret of the Compass

*K*nowing Emily, Jack thought, as he and Scott waited for her in the kitchen of The Lighthouse, *she has some kind of high-tech secret agent gadget specially designed for taking prints from compass concretions.* So he was more than a little surprised when she returned with a box covered in pictures of Disney princesses.

'Ta-da!' she announced. 'It was a Christmas present

from my cousins. It's been sitting in my bedroom cupboard for years.' She opened the box, tossed aside a wobbly rubber Cinderella mould and pulled out a bag of white powder. 'It's a model-making kit.'

Scott grinned as he took the bag. 'Plaster of Paris. Just the thing!' He began measuring out water and stirring in the powder while Jack covered the table with old newspaper. Emily gently cleaned away loose sand from the inner surfaces of the two 'shells' with a damp cloth, then carefully poured in the thin white mixture. She tapped the casings to remove air bubbles and balanced them on egg boxes to set.

Scott checked the instructions. 'Leave to set for at least twelve hours.'

'Twelve whole hours!' Jack groaned. 'I'll have died of suspense by then!'

〜

Somehow, Jack survived the night in spite of the suspense. Next morning he and Scott raced to The Lighthouse to join Emily for the official unmoulding.

With trembling fingers, Emily tried to ease the solid plaster of Paris away from the casings. Then she tried prising it off with a knife, poking it with a skewer and pulling it with tongs. It was no good. The plaster was stuck fast.

Jack shrugged. 'We'll just have to break the casing off.' He looked around for a suitable implement and found a big wooden mallet Emily's mum used for tenderizing steaks.

'*Noooo!*' Scott leaped round the table and grabbed Jack's arm before he could strike. 'Don't do that!'

Jack laughed. 'So you'd rather just sit around looking at two useless lumps of plaster?'

Emily looked from Jack to Scott. If the plaster crumbled when they broke the casing they wouldn't have another chance to get it right. But without breaking the casing, they'd never know the secret of Thomas Pendragon's compass.

At last, she nodded at Jack.

'OK,' Scott sighed. 'But at least let's use a little *finesse!*' He put the meat mallet back in the drawer and returned with a teaspoon. Gingerly, he tapped the casing until it shattered like the shell of a boiled egg. Emily peeled away the tiny pieces with tweezers.

At last, an octagonal block of white plaster emerged. The domed upper surface was printed with an intricate design of intersecting lines.

'It's just more of that stupid pattern,' Jack said in disgust.

Emily opened her notebook to the printout she'd made from Kelly's video. Jack was right. The patterns matched exactly.

'Maybe the map's on the other half of the casing,'

Scott said, beginning the painstaking boiled-egg-peeling process all over again.

But instead of a map, the new cast revealed just five words in the centre. Emily held it up to the window to get more light.

'*For You Cross My Ear,*' Jack read aloud over her shoulder. 'What's *that* supposed to mean?'

Scott peered at the faint words stamped into the chalky surface. The spacing was uneven. It looked as if there were some other letters that hadn't come out well enough to see. 'We need cocoa,' he announced.

Jack stared at his brother. 'We're about to crack a vital clue and you want to stop for a hot chocolate break?'

Scott laughed. He took a pinch of cocoa powder and sprinkled it over the surface of the plaster. Then he blew across it. Most of the cocoa puffed up in a cloud, but a little of the powder remained lodged in the tiny grooves. Now the letters – including the missing ones – were traced in chocolate brown.

Forever Yours, Cross My Heart.

Emily groaned and stared gloomily at the words on the plaster cast. 'It looks like this was just a romantic message. I remember when Old Bob told me the story of Thomas Pendragon, he said Pendragon's wife died very young and he was heartbroken. This must be in her memory.'

Scott couldn't hide his disappointment. 'But what

about the smugglers' hoard? Pendragon said in that letter that the directions were on the compass. Was he just bluffing in case the letter fell into the wrong hands?'

While Emily and Scott talked, Jack was unusually quiet. To the untrained eye, he may have looked as if he was staring into space, but his brain was working overtime. *This just doesn't add up,* he thought. *Old Thomas Pendragon was an intrepid smuggler – just like my Carter ancestors.* So what was he doing wearing a compass that was little more than an oversized necklace, with a message like something off a soppy Valenetine's card on one side and a load of curly-wurly patterns on the other? It had to be a trick to make people *think* it was just some lovey-dovey rubbish, when really it was . . . what? A secret map or a hidden code? Jack glared at the pattern on the plaster cast. It didn't look like a map of anything – apart from a maze, of course!

Yeah, right! he thought. *Like there's just going to be a centuries-old maze conveniently located in Castle Key!*

But, wait! There *was* an old maze on the island: a huge complicated maze, constructed from thick green yew hedges. He'd seen it when they were on the trail of the Midnight Ghost last summer.

And what had Mrs White said when he was helping with the fudge-tasting? *There was an old story that*

125

*the smugglers' hiding place was somewhere on the
Pendragon Estate itself.*

'Of course!' he cried.

'Of course, what?' Scott demanded.

Jack jumped out of his chair and did a lap of honour
round the kitchen, then held up the plaster cast. 'I think
you'll find this is no ordinary pattern. It is a map of the
maze at Pendragon Manor!'

Emily was silent for a moment, her mouth opening
and closing. Then she did some victory laps of her own.
'Jack, you're a genius!' she cheered. 'Pendragon wasn't
just being romantic. He meant cross the heart of the
maze. What better hiding place could there be?'

Scott joined Emily and Jack, dancing round, chanting.
'We've got the map! We're going to find the hoard!'
He grabbed two jars of pasta to use as maracas. 'Jack
Carter,' he laughed, 'you're the Man of the Match!' For
once, Scott didn't even have to remind himself of the
Shark Deal to be nice to his brother.

Drift barked happily and sped round and round the
table chasing his tail.

Emily's dad put his head round the door. 'Keep the
noise down, kids. We've got guests, you know!' He
glanced at Scott's makeshift maracas. 'Practising for a
carnival parade?'

'Something like that,' Emily giggled.

Jack grinned wickedly. 'We're going to dress Scott up
in sequins and a feather headdress.' He braced himself

for a kick on the shin or a punch on the arm but it didn't come. Really, what was going on with Scott these days?

As soon as Mr Wild left, Emily became serious again. 'There's no time to lose. If *we've* figured out that this is a map of the maze at Pendragon Manor, the compass-thief might have done too. We've got to get there first!'

Fifteen

Into the Maze

Before long, Jack, Scott and Emily were propping their bikes against a giant oak in the woods that surrounded Pendragon Manor on the west coast of Castle Key. Drift hopped down from his basket on the back of Emily's bike and trotted behind them along the path that wound its way through a sea of bluebells. Moments later they arrived at a tall hedge and peeped through to the landscaped gardens.

Beyond the sweeping lawns, a grand staircase guarded by stone lions led up to a terrace and the Tudor mansion itself.

The rambling old house, with its deeply sloping roofs, huge chimneys and diamond-leaded windows, was no longer occupied by the Pendragon family, but was now a popular venue for weddings and conferences. The house and grounds were also open to the public on certain days of the week. Emily had checked the website before they left and unfortunately this wasn't one of them. But there'd been a unanimous vote: there was no way they could wait until next Thursday, the next day the house was open to the public, to explore the maze for the smugglers' hiding place.

Which was why Jack was now gaining entry to the garden by commando crawling under the hedge rather than walking through the main gate. He poked his head out through the branches for a recce. He could hear distant chatter and the clink of glasses. There was a party of men in suits and ladies in brightly coloured dresses up on the terrace. But the rest of the garden was empty. 'All clear!' he hissed.

Emily, Scott and Drift squeezed through the hedge and darted across the vast expanse of lawn, like soldiers crossing no man's land. They threw themselves into the cover of the maze.

'Phase One accomplished,' Emily whispered, pulling the map from her bag. Before they'd set out, Scott had used his cocoa technique to darken the pattern on the plaster, photographed it, enlarged the image and printed it out. Then he'd pasted in the small missing section at the edge from the printout of Kelly's video.

Emily consulted the diagram, pointing to an opening in the outer line. 'This must be the entrance,' she hissed. There was something about the silent stillness within the ancient maze that made them all whisper.

'Which means it's this way!' Jack turned left and marched confidently between the towering walls of dark dense foliage.

After more than an hour in the maze they still hadn't found the centre. Scott and Jack were arguing about whether they should have taken a right instead of a left three turns back. Emily was wondering whether they'd made a massive mistake. Maybe the pattern on the compass wasn't a map of the maze after all. And, she realized, if the piece of paper she was clutching in her hand wasn't a map into the maze, it wasn't a map *out* of it either!

She was starting to think they'd be wandering among the dark hedges all day when Drift flicked up his ears and ran on ahead. She chased after him round a hairpin bend and came out in a circular clearing.

'The heart of the maze!' Emily breathed.

'Awesome!' Jack shouted, breaking out of a whisper for the first time. He turned to Scott who was just behind him. 'Told you we were on the right track.'

Excitedly, the three friends began to search for the smugglers' hoard. There was a brass plaque set into the grass in the middle, but no amount of pressing or pulling revealed a hidden entrance. They were starting to investigate the wooden bench that ran around the edge of the clearing when a loud angry voice made them all jump.

'What do you kids think you're doing?'

Scott looked up to see a man the size of a buffalo glaring down at them. His huge head was topped with tight coppery curls and his neck disappeared into muscle-bound shoulders.

Oh, no! It's the compass-thief, Scott thought. *He's looking for the smugglers' hoard too. We might as well give up now. We don't stand a chance against this giant!* But then he noticed a badge pinned to the man's green overalls: *Dan Holworthy, Gardener.* It was OK. He just worked here. And surely gardeners were nice gentle people who liked growing things . . .

'The grounds aren't open to the public today!' the gardener roared, looking anything *but* gentle.

'We're with the party,' Jack said nervously. 'Just having a look round.'

The gardener eyed him suspiciously. 'You're attending the Cornish Sausage Manufacturers' Annual Conference?'

'Er, yeah, we were invited because we're . . .' Jack's

voice tailed off. What would they be doing at a sausage convention?

'Because we're their best customers,' Emily piped up. 'We're special guests.'

'Mmm, *sausages*,' Scott free-formed. 'Can't get enough of them!'

Drift wagged his tail. *Sausages* was one of his favourite words. He just couldn't figure out why everyone kept saying it when there wasn't even the slightest whiff of a sausage in the air.

The grumpy gardener wasn't happy. 'Well, the maze is out of bounds. And if I catch you lot trespassing again, you'll feel my boot under your backsides!' He kicked the air with a gargantuan hobnailed boot to demonstrate. 'I'm pruning in here and I can't have members of the public wandering around.'

'What was *his* problem?' Scott grumbled as they slunk back to the lawn. 'Anyone would think we'd broken into Buckingham Palace!'

'More to the point, what was he *up to*?' Emily murmured.

'Pruning,' Jack said. 'He told us.'

'Oh, yeah!' Emily snorted. 'Where were his shears then?'

Jack shrugged.

Scott thought for a moment. 'You're right! And we'd have heard him snipping away if he'd *really* been pruning.'

'So what do we do now?' Jack asked.

'Simple,' Emily said. 'You can't garden at night. We'll wait till he's gone home and try again.'

—

Emily, Scott, Jack and Drift established a stake-out position behind a magnolia bush near the staff car park and – sustained only by Jack's pack of emergency jelly beans – waited until they spotted Dan Holworthy climbing into an old jeep, revving the engine and roaring off down the road towards Tregower.

Then they crept back across the lawn and into the maze.

It was early evening by now. The corridors between the tall yew hedges were steeped in shadow. The friends swiftly retraced their steps through the twists and turns and arrived at the centre of the labyrinth.

'There has to be a trapdoor down here *somewhere*,' Emily whispered, crawling under the circular bench.

Drift had no idea what they were looking for, but he joined the search too. He never turned down the chance of a really good snuffle around old tree roots, although these yews were a bit disappointing. There were no scent-mark updates to read, because dogs – ordinary dogs, who weren't assisting their owner on special operations, that was – weren't allowed in the maze. A hint of a squirrel trail mixed with boot leather wafted past Drift's nose. He burrowed further into the bottom of the hedge to investigate. When he came out on the other side, he found himself in a small grassy area surrounded on all sides by more of those dark, creepy hedges that made his fur stand on end. As he turned to go back, his paw caught on something in the grass. But when he tried to pick it up in his teeth it wouldn't budge. *Hmm, Emily might be interested in this . . .*

On the other side of the hedge, Emily heard an Alert Bark. She looked up from under the bench but her Right Hand Dog was nowhere to be seen. She heard a second bark. It was coming from the other side of the hedge, yet there was no gap in the solid wall of yew. 'Drift's stuck on the other side!' she cried.

'Don't worry, I'll find him!' Jack charged at the hedge in a high-speed shoulder barge.

Emily's hands flew to her face. The dense mesh of branches and twigs had been trained to come right down to the ground to prevent people breaking through to cheat their way to the centre of the maze. She waited for Jack's cries as he became caught up and scratched to ribbons in the thick hedge.

But, to her surprise, he simply disappeared.

Sixteen

The Hoard

Scott and Emily looked at the hedge and then at each other. One minute Jack was there, the next he'd vanished.

Scott inspected the hedge. This section had been carefully clipped to look like a thick barrier of interlocking branches, just like the rest of the maze, but it was, in fact, woven out of smaller twigs and leaves. It gave way at the slightest touch. He pushed his arm into the foliage, almost punching his brother on the nose as Jack poked his head back through.

'Come and look at this,' Jack laughed.

Emily pushed through the leaves. She was standing in a secret room at the heart of the maze and there, poking out of the grass, was a ring of black iron. She knelt and hugged Drift. He really was the cleverest dog ever!

Then she began scraping away the earth and grass. Drift and the boys joined in and soon they revealed a solid wooden trapdoor.

'I was right,' Emily breathed. 'This is it!'

'What are we waiting for?' Jack grabbed the handle and heaved with all his might. The trapdoor creaked open.

Emily pulled her torch from her bag and shone it down into the hole.

A flight of roughly hewn steps led down into a tunnel.

'Do you think we should go in?' Scott cautioned. 'It might be dangerous.'

Emily and Jack stared at him.

'Are you joking?' Emily asked. 'We're *that* close to finding Pendragon's hiding place!'

Scott followed them down the steps. For once he was glad Jack and Emily hadn't listened to him. He was just as impatient to find the hoard as they were!

The tunnel was dark and cold, barely wide enough to walk in single file. Jack stooped under the low roof and felt his way along the damp wall, following the light of Emily's torch. Cobwebs brushed against the back of his neck. He shuddered. There were probably all kinds of giant, mutant two-hundred-year-old spiders lurking in this underground lair . . .

Suddenly Emily stopped. Jack walked into her, tripping over Drift. Scott bumped into him.

'The tunnel's opening out,' Emily said, sweeping her torch beam from side to side. 'I'm sure we're getting close.'

In the gloom Jack began to make out heaps of objects piled up against the walls. He forgot all about mutant spiders. The Smuggling Carter blood was singing in his veins. He could sniff out contraband with his smuggler's sixth sense . . . Barrels of rum and brandy, chests of silver doubloons, sacks overflowing with exotic spices . . .

He looked closer at the piles of swag.

This wasn't right! Where were the old barrels and chests? Where were the brandy and doubloons? 'Er, did they have DVDs in the eighteenth century?' he asked, picking up a copy of *Toy Story 2* with Chinese writing on the cover.

'Of course they didn't!' Emily snapped.

'They didn't have fake designer trainers either,' Scott said, taking a box from a pile and examining the logo.

They all stood in silence. The pool of light from Emily's torch revealed heap upon heap of DVDs, computer games, mobile phones, perfumes, trainers, cigarettes, Manchester United football shirts . . .

Scott reached for a copy of the new computer game he'd been eagerly awaiting for months. 'This one's not even out yet. It must be a pirate copy. And those Man U shirts aren't the real thing either!'

Jack kicked a pile of satnavs, sending them clattering to the ground. He picked one up and examined the date on the back: August 2008. 'Some wheeler-dealer has been stashing their knock-off goods down here for years. No wonder that trapdoor opened so easily!'

Emily had never felt so disappointed in her entire life. This wasn't the hoard of an eighteenth-century smuggling ring. It was just a pile of modern – and very dodgy – merchandise. She gulped down the lump in her throat. She was *not* going to cry in front of the boys.

Suddenly Drift sat up with his ears trembling. Then they all heard it: footsteps were ringing out in the tunnel. And they were getting closer.

Emily glanced round to see a shadow on the tunnel wall. It was the shape of a man – but the size of an ogre! Frantically, she looked around. Where could they hide? She noticed another tunnel opening behind the Man U shirts. 'Quick!' she whispered, and ran towards it, switching off her torch as she went.

As he followed, Jack looked back over his shoulder

and glimpsed the gardener, Dan Holworthy, lumbering into the storage area, his features distorted like a Halloween pumpkin by the light of his lamp. He dumped the box of satellite dishes he was carrying, noticed the toppled stack of satnavs, and held up his lamp to look around.

The friends pelted along the tunnel, stumbling and bumping into each other in the dark. At last they came to a flight of steps, and tumbled up them like a pile of dominoes. They could hear the footsteps in the tunnel behind them growing louder and louder.

Emily switched on her torch for a moment. There was a small door up ahead. Jack dived for the handle.

'What are you doing?' Scott gasped. 'You don't know what's on the other side!'

'Well, if you want to stay here for a friendly chat with Holworthy, feel free!' Jack hissed. 'I'm not. You heard what he said about boots and backsides! And that was just for going in the maze. Now we've discovered his secret stash of goodies, he's really going to lose it!'

Jack pushed the door open a crack. Blinking in the bright light, he took in a polished wooden floor, gleaming oak panelling and walls full of old portraits.

'It's the entrance hall at Pendragon Manor,' Emily whispered behind him. 'We've come out under the main staircase.'

Jack nodded. They'd been here several times last summer when investigating the kidnap of a famous film star. *Let's hope we can get out without being intercepted by Bossy Bailey,* he thought, remembering the tyrannical housekeeper.

The footsteps in the tunnel behind them were growing louder.

Jack was about to burst through the door, when Mrs Bailey stepped into the hall. Her smart blue skirt, beige tights and sensible brown shoes parked themselves right in front of the door under the stairs – and in front of Jack's nose.

'Pre-dinner drinks and nibbles are served in the hall,' she announced to the throng of sausage manufacturers who followed her.

The footsteps behind them were so close that Jack could hear the squeak of boot leather. Any second now Holworthy would charge round the last bend in the tunnel and see them.

With seconds to spare, Mrs Bailey moved aside. Jack, Emily, Scott and Drift piled out into the midst of the noisy conference crowd and elbowed their way through. Jack barely had time to grab a handful of cocktail sausages from a waiter's silver tray before they bolted down the corridor past the kitchen, out of the back door, through the vegetable garden and over the wall into the woods.

Next day, when the friends gathered at Stone Cottage, they were so downcast that even Aunt Kate's Victoria sponge couldn't cheer them up. They'd found the smugglers' hiding place but it was a worthless triumph!

Like scoring a winning goal in the last minute of a cup final, then the referee calling it offside, Scott thought. Holworthy must have stumbled across the trapdoor when he was working in the maze and realized that the old tunnel was the perfect hideaway for all his fell-off-the-back-of-a-lorry goods. No wonder he'd been so keen to shoo the friends away yesterday. And no doubt if Holworthy had found any of the original smugglers' contraband down there, he'd have sold anything of value years ago.

Emily could hardly even face writing up her notes. She flung her notebook down on the grass – it was a sunny morning and they were sitting outside in the garden. Operation Compass had reached a dead end. 'I suppose we ought to call D. I. Hassan and tell him about Holworthy's hoard,' she said half-heartedly. 'Some of that stuff could be stolen property.'

'It's so frustrating! We still don't know what happened to the compass,' Scott complained. 'I'm sure Holworthy didn't steal it from the wreck. Even if he can scuba dive, how would he have known it was down there?'

'And why would he want the compass anyway?' Jack pointed out. 'He wouldn't have needed the map if he'd already found the hoard years ago.'

There was something else that was bothering Jack too. 'Mrs White said that Thomas Pendragon was meant to be this super-smart smuggler who fooled the revenue men for years – almost as smart as the Carters of Prussia Cove,' he couldn't resist adding, 'so how come he put such a no-brainer of a clue on his compass? A map of the maze in his own front garden and directions saying *Look in the Middle Bit*. It's not rocket science, is it? It's like putting a sign up outside your house saying *Burglars This Way!*'

Emily chewed her pen. 'Yeah, that is a bit odd. Maybe it was a bluff. You know, people would think it was so obvious that they wouldn't bother to look there?'

'First rule of bluffing!' Aunt Kate's voice made the friends jump. She was reclining in a deckchair on the patio nearby with *The Carrickstowe Times* propped over her face. They'd all assumed she was fast asleep. 'If something *seems* too obvious, it almost certainly *is* too obvious.'

'What do you mean?' Jack asked.

Aunt Kate sat up and looked over the newspaper. 'Distraction,' she said. 'Just like a magician. You wave a big silk handkerchief over here. Meanwhile you're hiding the coin over there with the other hand. Everyone's so busy looking at the hanky they don't see the coin. Same with codes. That big shiny map of the maze may have been intended to blind people to the real clue. Oldest trick in the book!'

'So you think . . .' Scott began. But Aunt Kate was already hurrying inside to the kitchen where her oven timer was beeping, her unruly white hair flying out from a forest of hairclips. Scott had already come to suspect that Aunt Kate wasn't your average old lady, but how did she know so much about code-breaking?

Emily snatched up her notebook, her spark suddenly reignited. 'Aunt Kate's right! What if that tunnel from the maze to the house was just a dummy to fool people into *thinking* they'd found the hiding place? Maybe Thomas Pendragon's *real* hoard was hidden somewhere completely different.'

'Like where?' Jack asked. The maze connection had been his stroke of genius. He was taking all this *dummy* talk as a personal insult.

Scott thought for a moment. 'Let's go back to the clue: *Forever Yours, Cross My Heart.* If it's not about the heart of the maze, what is it about?'

Emily began brainstorming ideas. 'Heart? That could be love? Maybe Pendragon's wife? The one who died young. The cross could mean a crucifix. What about a cross in a church?'

'Would they be allowed to have a hiding place in a church?' Scott asked.

Jack nodded. 'The smugglers often built tunnels under churches.'

'How do *you* know?' Scott demanded.

'I read it in that book from the library,' Jack said.

'You'd be surprised what you can learn in a book!' he added smugly. 'They even built them under family tombs sometimes.'

Scott and Emily looked at Jack. They were back in business – the church in Castle Key was only moments away from Stone Cottage!

Seventeen

The Graveyard Trail

Jack had always thought graveyards were creepy, but the one at St Michael's was peaceful and sort of friendly. You could hear the sea rolling in the background and the bees buzzing about in the wild flowers that grew among the long grass. Along with Scott and Emily, he searched for names on the old headstones, scattered in higgledy-piggledy groups under the chestnut trees and lilacs, weathered by wind and sea-salt and richly embroidered with moss and lichen. All the old Castle Key families were gathered there: Trevithicks and Cuttances, Lovedays and Kerrows, Whites and Tragos . . .

But there were no Pendragons.

'Can I help you?'

Jack turned to see the curate, Colin Warnock, strolling down the steps from the church, his crest of purple hair glowing in the bright sunlight. Colin waved goodbye to the bell-ringing group he'd been leading and joined the friends, who were gazing down at the grave of a seventeenth-century doctor.

Jack could see Emily and Scott both racking their brains for the perfect reason to ask Colin about the location of the Pendragon family tomb, without giving away the nature of their investigation. But Jack was too impatient to bother with subterfuge. Colin could be trusted; he'd helped them before *and* he'd shown Jack how to play the *Star Wars* theme on the church organ last summer. Jack opted for the direct approach. 'We're trying to find the Pendragon family tomb.'

Colin smiled. 'Ah, well you won't find it here. The Pendragons had their own chapel on the estate, tucked away in the woods. It's abandoned now, of course, but all the old family graves would be there.'

He was still talking as the three friends shouted their thanks and darted out of the graveyard.

'To the bikes!' Jack cried as they rocketed into Church Lane. 'Let's go find ourselves a chapel.'

But suddenly Emily's face fell. 'Oh, no! I've just had a text from Mum. I've got to go and help her with the spring cleaning.'

Scott grimaced at Jack. 'That reminds me. We promised we'd help Aunt Kate do a big supermarket shop in Carrickstowe this afternoon. We have to carry the bags home on the bus for her.'

Emily checked her watch. 'OK, we'll go this evening. Rendezvous here at eighteen hundred hours.'

'Ah, just the guys I was looking for!' The friends looked up to see Joe Gordon hurrying up the lane.

Scott shuffled nervously. The last time he'd seen Joe Gordon, the man had been brandishing a green plastic Scooby-Doo compass and having a meltdown about silly time-wasting pranks. But he needn't have worried. Joe shook his hand and patted his back.

'I got back from Bristol this morning. It seems I owe you an apology, Scott. Kelly's shown me the footage from her video camera. You *did* see the Pendragon compass on the wreck. I should never have accused you of playing tricks.'

'It's OK,' Scott mumbled.

'I was so gutted about the compass not being there, I wasn't thinking straight,' Joe went on. Then he smiled. 'Anyway, I'm giving a talk all about the *Mermaid* dive to the local community this evening and I'd like you

– and Emily and Jack of course – to be the guests of honour. It's in the Great Hall at Pendragon Manor. I hope you can come.'

Scott thanked Joe politely for the invitation.

'Drat!' Emily said through her teeth as Joe left. 'Now we'll have to wait until tomorrow to look for the chapel.'

The talk started out OK, Jack thought. Joe Gordon explained that he was diving down to the *Mermaid* to recover treasure for the Pendragon Estate. He showed the audience some cool pictures of divers exploring wrecks in exciting places like Egypt and Vanuatu.

Then Joe praised Scott for having spotted an important artefact on the wreck. Jack sighed. You could practically *see* Scott's head inflating like a balloon. If Joe said another word, it might actually explode! Joe also talked about Emily's bravery in saving Kelly's life. Kelly whooped 'Go, girl!' and everyone clapped. Emily tried to look modest. Just when Jack was muttering to himself about not getting a mention, he heard his name.

'Jack Carter and Kelly Mann have been doing some great work tracing family connections back to the heyday of smuggling in Cornwall,' Joe said, and there was a round of applause. Jack looked down, trying not to catch Mrs White's eye; she was sitting in the next row.

Maybe he should have just mentioned to Kelly that Mrs White helped him a bit with that family tree.

After that, the lecture went downhill. Joe Gordon started going on about what kind of wood the *Mermaid* was built from and how many nails the carpenters had used. Jack zoned out and gazed around the hall. *Who wanted to know this stuff?*

After what seemed like hours, Joe announced a short break for refreshments. Everyone flocked around Scott and Emily, wanting to hear all about their diving adventures. Jack slunk away from the crowds. He saw Mrs White approaching. Backing away in case she wanted to know why he'd taken all the credit for her research, he accidentally stood on Mrs Loveday's foot. Mrs Loveday began telling everyone how Jack had mugged her for a chocolate cake. Mrs Bailey the bossy housekeeper shot him a suspicious look from behind the drinks table. Had she clocked him escaping from the tunnel under the stairs during the sausage convention yesterday?

Feeling like Public Enemy Number One, Jack sidled towards the door.

He had to get out of here!

Suddenly he had one of his brainwaves. Instead of going back in for the second half of the boring lecture, *why not go and look for the chapel?* True, it was pitch dark out there, but if the chapel was somewhere in the grounds of the manor, it couldn't be too far away. It'd be silly *not* to just have a quick look while he was here.

He slipped out though the back door.

—

Jack ran to the car park and took the front light from his bike to use as a torch. Then he backtracked to the kitchen garden. At first it was easy. Light spilled from the windows of the manor and splashed across the greenhouses, wigwams of beanpoles and raspberry canes. There was a hairy moment when a scarecrow loomed out of the shadows, but Jack hurried past and hopped over the wall.

Then he was swallowed up by the dark woods.

As Jack hurried along the path through the trees, his bike light picked out twisted branches like long bony fingers, what looked like faces leering out from gnarled tree trunks, and the faint shimmies of leaves as unseen creatures scurried into the undergrowth. Once the light reflected back from a pair of watchful eyes: a fox or a badger, perhaps?

Or an evil goblin?

Owls hooted from the trees. Except they didn't go *too-whit, too-whoo* like they did in story books. They howled like the ghosts of demented monkeys.

Ghosts!

Suddenly Jack remembered that Pendragon Manor was haunted.

I don't believe in ghosts, he reminded himself.

But there were a lot of things Jack didn't *officially* believe in that were suddenly starting to seem very real indeed as he ventured deeper and deeper into the dark woods: ghouls, vampires, orcs, werewolves and trolls to name but a few. And now he thought he heard footsteps padding along behind. But whenever he stopped to listen, the phantom stalker stopped too. All he could hear was his heart banging in his ears.

Maybe this hadn't been such a great idea.

Joe Gordon's talk hadn't been *that* boring.

It'd make much more sense to search for the chapel in the morning light.

Jack turned and jogged back along the path. It was getting cold now. He could see his breath and his lungs were rasping. Fog was starting to settle among the trees on either side of the path.

He came to a fork and stopped.

Which way had he come?

Eighteen

Cross My Heart

J ack picked a direction at random and headed down the left hand path. But he didn't remember seeing that enormous tree stump before, or that broken gate sticking up out of the undergrowth. He turned back. But the other path didn't look familiar either.

Panic rising in his chest, Jack stumbled on. Roots caught his feet, brambles snatched at his legs. The path became more and more overgrown until it wasn't even a proper path any more and he was fighting his way through bushes and brambles.

Suddenly, Jack's hand bumped against something solid. He tore away handfuls of ivy to find that he was standing in front of a heavy wooden door, studded with metal rivets.

He pulled down more ivy to reveal a huge metal doorknob.

Jack turned the knob. He put his shoulder to the door and pushed.

Who knew what was on the other side? But nothing could be worse than wandering the woods alone.

The hinges creaked.

Jack stepped through the door.

Stone arches, wooden pews, crosses on the walls, candlesticks dripping with melted wax . . . This had to be the Pendragon chapel!

For a moment, Jack's fear was squeezed out by excitement.

But then he saw two dead bodies.

An explosion of terror ripped through his body. The bike light clattered to the floor. Startled by the noise, bats fluttered from every corner and flew out through a broken stained glass window.

Jack fumbled for the bike light. Hardly daring to look, or even breathe, he aimed the light in the direction of the bodies. Draped in long robes, they lay side by side on their backs, hands together in prayer, skin deathly pale, eyes vacant.

Slowly Jack inched closer. He almost laughed with relief.

The bodies were carved from stone on top of an enormous rectangular tomb. Jack knelt and read the inscriptions on the side.

WILLIAM PENDRAGON 1589-1642
JOSIAH PENDRAGON 1650-1721

'Oh, yeah, Jack Carter triumphs again!' Jack shouted, completely forgetting that he was lost in a spooky deserted chapel in the middle of a dark wood. He couldn't wait to see Scott and Emily's faces when he told them that, while they were listening to Joe waffling about eighteenth-century ship-building techniques, he'd single-handedly discovered the Pendragon family tomb!

Now all he had to do was find the secret hiding place and he'd have bagged the smugglers' hoard too!

But where was the hidden entrance? This tomb was a solid great lump of stone.

Jack walked round the tomb and found another body lying all alone. The beautiful young woman was so lifelike she almost seemed to breathe, her pale stone features glowing in the beam of the bike light. Her hands were folded across her chest and she held a small cross in her long white fingers. She looked like an angel.

How could she have died so young? Jack wondered.

Suddenly he was reminded of something Emily had said when they were making the plaster casts from the compass casings: *Pendragon's wife died very young.* Could this be her? Jack searched and found a plaque beneath the woman's tiny feet.

ELIZABETH PENDRAGON 1733-1754

Jack strained his brain to remember the year Thomas Pendragon's ship, the *Mermaid*, had run aground. He was sure it was 1779. The dates worked!

There was something else written on the plaque too: *Forever Yours*. A shiver ran down Jack's spine. He'd seen those words before, traced out in cocoa powder on plaster. The words on Elizabeth's tomb were engraved on the Pendragon compass. The secret entrance had to be here. He tried pressing on the words, sliding the plaque to one side, pushing on the scrolls of stone carving around it, but nothing worked.

Jack was ready to burst with frustration. So near and yet so far! And now his bike light was dwindling as the battery ran down. He was going to have to try to find his way back through the woods before it failed altogether. He gazed down at the serene face of Elizabeth Pendragon, as if expecting her to wake up and whisper the secret to him.

But then he realized. She didn't need to.

He'd figured it out for himself.

The cross Elizabeth held in her hands pointed directly to her heart!

Cross My Heart – those were the other words on the compass! Jack reached out and touched the cross, gently tracing his fingers over the cold stone.

The side of the tomb slid back, crunching over the bat droppings on the stone floor. At the same time the door of the chapel creaked open.

Jack glanced up to see a tall, shadowy figure standing in the doorway.

Dan Holworthy!

What was the Gardener from Hell doing in the deserted chapel at night? Jack wasn't going to hang around to find out. He ducked inside the tomb and slid the panel closed behind him.

Nineteen

Into the Crypt

As soon as the panel closed behind him Jack had second thoughts.

He was inside a crypt!

Crypts were full of dead bodies!

He tried to push the panel open again. He'd rather climb back out and take his chances with Holworthy's boot. But the panel wouldn't move. It was stuck fast.

Jack just had time to glimpse a shelf full of grinning

skulls before his bike light flickered and went out. The battery was dead. *Like everything else in here!*

He banged his fists on the wall. He screamed for help. Nothing happened.

HE WAS BURIED ALIVE!

Jack sank to the ground. The darkness was so black it was suffocating. He tried closing his eyes and then opening them. It made no difference. He was afraid to move in case he bumped into those skulls. Or something even worse. He was freezing cold. And he didn't even have any emergency jelly beans left.

And now he was starting to hallucinate! The shadowy figure he'd seen in the chapel doorway kept flashing into his mind as if it were trying to tell him something. He realized that the figure hadn't been beefy like Holworthy at all, but tall and gangly. More like Theo Jarvis, in fact . . . but why would Theo be in the chapel?

And just when Jack thought things couldn't get any worse, he felt something tickling his knee.

Spider!

Then he heard claws scratching on the stone floor.

Rats!

And then he felt something nuzzle his hand.

Rats don't nuzzle! he thought. *Nor do spiders.*

'Drift!' Jack sobbed, burying his face in Drift's warm fur, inhaling the comforting smell of damp dog. 'It's you!'

Drift licked Jack's nose. He had no idea what Jack was up to, but when he'd seen him creep out of the big house and set off into the woods all alone he'd thought he'd better keep an eye on him. Emily had left him on Lookout Duty, as dogs weren't allowed inside the manor. Jack was a great young pup, but he was a lot like a labrador; obsessed with food, full of enthusiasm, and always getting into trouble. He was Drift's favourite human (after Emily, of course) but when it came to thinking things through, Jack could be two biscuits short of a full bowl at times. So Drift had followed him through the woods to keep an eye on him. It was more fun than sitting outside the manor waiting for Emily too! He kept his distance just in case Jack was on some kind of Undercover Stealth Mission, and followed him into the old building. He'd suspected that crawling into this big stone box was not one of Jack's better ideas, but he'd slipped in behind him anyway.

Drift lifted his nose and sniffed. On top of the delectable earthy-ratty-bony smells, he could detect a trace of fresh air coming in from somewhere. Just as he thought – there was a tunnel leading off from the other side of this underground space. Of course, he was going to have to herd Jack along. Jack's light seemed to have disappeared and it was well known that humans couldn't see in the dark. And as for following scents? No chance! Their noses were about as much use as a cat's tail.

Drift nudged Jack's hand, then trotted a little way along the tunnel, barked softly and waited for him to follow.

Jack struggled to his feet, banged his head on the roof, ducked, and shuffled blindly in the direction of Drift's bark.

Eventually, Drift came to a dead end. Oddly, he was now picking up human food smells rather than fresh air, but there was a round metal door set into the wall, with what looked like some kind of handle. He nudged Jack. One thing humans *were* good at was handles!

The sliver of light leaking in round the edge of the door was just bright enough for Jack to make out a bolt. He gave it a shove. It was very stiff but finally it shot back with a clang. Jack tugged on the handle and for the third time in two days, opened a door into the unknown.

This time he found himself standing in a charred metal basket inside an enormous brick structure the size of a small room. It opened out into a vast area of white tile and stainless steel, bristling with racks of knives and strange devices with gleaming blades. He seemed to have stepped into the secret laboratory of an evil scientist!

Then he realized that one of the machines was a fancy cake mixer and another was a ham slicer.

He was in the old Tudor fireplace in the kitchen of Pendragon Manor.

Meanwhile, Scott and Emily were searching for Jack. Joe Gordon's talk was finally over. Mr and Mrs White had offered to give the friends – and their bikes – a lift back to Castle Key village in their Land Rover.

'Typical!' Scott muttered. 'Disappeared, just when you need him.'

'Maybe he's gone to find Drift,' Emily suggested, heading for the back door where she'd left him on Lookout Duty.

They were halfway down the corridor when two figures shot out from the kitchen, swathed in cobwebs and smothered in dust and soot.

Emily shrank back in shock.

'What happened to you two?' Scott asked. 'You look like a pair of zombies!'

'I've only found the Pendragon chapel!' Jack blurted. 'And the family tomb. And a tunnel. Aunt Kate was right. The maze was a decoy.'

Emily stared at him, trying to make sense of the torrent of words. 'Did you find the smugglers' hoard?' she demanded.

Jack frowned, making white creases across his sooty forehead. 'Well, er, no! I don't know.'

Scott snorted. 'You found the tunnel but you *forgot* to look for the treasure?'

Jack waved his lifeless bike light in Scott's face. 'It was dark down there. I could have walked past the mask of Tutankhamen and the Crown Jewels and I wouldn't have noticed. If it hadn't been for Drift I'd never have found my way out.' He bent to give Drift a big hug. 'He's an awesome guide dog!'

Scott was about to point out just how idiotic it had been to enter a dark crypt in the first place when he remembered his Shark Deal again. 'Fair enough,' he said. 'Good work. We'll come back tomorrow morning for a proper look.'

Jack blinked in surprise. Did Scott really just say *good work*? Then he remembered something else. 'Someone came into the chapel. I don't know whether he saw me, but he didn't follow me into the tunnel. I would have heard him.'

Emily was outraged. 'Holworthy! That thug! He's got his own hiding place. He's not getting his hands on *our* smugglers' hoard as well. Come on! Let's get back down there now.'

Jack shook his head. 'That's the weird part. I thought it was Holworthy at first, but I'm pretty sure it was Theo Jarvis!'

'Theo Jarvis?' Scott echoed.

Emily stared at Jack for a moment, then suddenly she grabbed him by the shoulders. 'Of course! Theo's the compass thief. We should have figured it out before. He works in a shop that hires diving kit. He's bound to know how to scuba dive. And the shop owns a jeep for transporting surf boards around. He could have driven down the track to Pirate Cove.'

Scott frowned at Emily. 'But how did he know about the compass? I didn't tell him about it when I hired my wetsuit.' Then he slapped his forehead and groaned. 'Oh, no, I think I've got it. That first day after the dive. We were having lunch outside Dotty's, talking about the compass. Theo was outside the Castle Key Cabin next door, putting out the display racks. He must have overheard us.'

Jack rolled his eyes. 'Yeah, I remember that. You two didn't stop banging on and on about the compass for ages. And Emily was asking you all about exactly where it was on the wreck. Anyone listening would have got precise directions on how to find it. But *why* would Theo want to steal it?'

'We'll worry about that later,' Scott answered. 'If Theo's got the compass he could work out the way into the tunnel any minute.'

'That's right,' Emily said, fishing in her bag for her torch. 'We've got to find the hoard first.'

'*Emily! Scott! Jack!*'

The friends turned to see Mrs White limping along the corridor, leaning on her stick. 'Ah, there you are. We've loaded the bikes already. Time to go!'

Emily turned to Scott and Jack. 'First thing tomorrow morning!' she whispered.

Scott nodded reluctantly.

'The crack of dawn,' Jack agreed. 'If not before,' he

added, glancing at Scott. He knew just how much his brother hated early mornings!

———

Next morning Jack led the way through the woods. Or, rather, Drift led the way, nose down, following last night's trail along the path. Jack walked alongside him, pretending he knew where he was going. Emily skipped along impatiently. Scott shuffled behind them like the walking dead. It *was* only six thirty a.m.!

When they reached the chapel, Jack swept out his arm like an estate agent taking customers round a show home. 'Look,' he said excitedly. 'It's got bats and everything!' He ushered them over to Elizabeth's tomb.

'Must have been a bit spooky in here by yourself last night,' Emily murmured.

Jack shrugged. 'Nah! I wasn't bothered!'

Together they all gazed down at Elizabeth Pendragon's beautiful, peaceful face.

'*Forever Yours,*' Scott murmured, reading the words on the plaque.

'*Cross My Heart,*' Emily whispered, pointing at the cross.

'So, how did you get the tomb to open?' Scott asked Jack.

Jack ran his fingers round the edge of the cross. 'Well, it was very complicated,' he said. 'It took a lot of figuring out of course, but eventually I cracked it.'

'Is something meant to happen?' Emily asked.

Jack jabbed at the cross. Still the side of the tomb didn't open.

Scott sighed. 'You were making the whole thing up, weren't you?'

Jack tried again, closing his eyes and trying desperately to remember exactly how he'd opened the tomb last night. He'd gently traced the shape with his fingers . . .

'It's moving!' Emily cried. 'The side's sliding back.'

'Leave it open a crack so we can get out again without having to go through the manor,' Emily said, crawling into the tomb with Drift.

Scott and Jack switched on their torches and followed.

'I think I preferred this place when I *couldn't* see,' Jack mumbled, trying not to look at the row upon row of skulls and skeletons neatly lined up in racks against the walls.

After walking for a few minutes, Scott noticed a tunnel off to the side. 'Maybe the hiding place is down here.' He ducked and entered the smaller tunnel.

Moments later the tunnel opened out and the friends stared in wonder – at piles of treasure!

Everything was smothered in dust and cobwebs, but the richness of the contraband beneath still shone through. Huge wooden chests and barrels were stacked on top of each other. Piles of silks and lace spilled over heaps of silver goblets and platters and sacks of spices and tobacco.

'Wow!' Emily breathed. 'I bet nobody has set eyes on this stuff for over two hundred years.'

That's when they heard someone running into the tunnel towards them.

'Oh, no!' Scott gasped. 'Theo must have found his way in.'

Jack whipped round and came face to face with the new arrival.

But it wasn't Theo Jarvis.

Twenty

Not Really Stealing

It was Dan Holworthy!

The giant gardener shone his torch at the friends and then at the pile of treasure, his eyes flicking between the two. 'Not bad!' he whistled.

'What are you doing here?' Scott demanded, trying to sound brave, even though Holworthy was wielding a large spade in a way that made it look more like a lethal weapon than a digging implement.

'Following you lot!' Holworthy laughed. 'I was trimming back some branches at the edge of the wood when I saw you sneak into the chapel. I thought I'd follow and see what you were up to. I'm glad I did now! I should get a good price for this old junk.'

Emily stepped next to Scott. 'It's not junk and you can't sell it.'

'Yeah!' Jack put in. 'This is smugglers' contraband.'

Holworthy pretended to shade his eyes and search around the tunnel. 'Well, I don't see any smugglers around to claim it, do you? Finders, keepers!'

'Well, *we* found it!' Scott pointed out. 'Not you!'

Holworthy shook his head. 'Which is why I'm going to have to tie you up! By the time anyone finds you down here I'll be long gone and so will this!' He waved his torch towards the treasure. 'Now, I just need to find some rope.'

Scott, Jack and Emily looked at each other in dismay as Holworthy backed towards the piles of booty, holding the spade out in front of him ready to strike if anyone moved. They couldn't believe that after all their work tracking down the smugglers' hoard, the treasure could be snatched from under their noses to be sold off in a car boot sale somewhere.

'Ah, here we are!' Holworthy bent to pick up a coil of rope from behind a barrel. But as he reached down Drift suddenly flew at him, baring his teeth and snarling. Taken by surprise, Holworthy dropped his torch.

'Quick!' Emily cried, grabbing Scott and Jack and pulling them with her. 'Come on, Drift!' Together they all darted past Holworthy, who was groping around on the floor for his torch, and bolted down the main tunnel.

'Keep going!' Jack panted. 'There's a door at the end of the tunnel. Follow Drift. He knows the way!'

Within seconds Holworthy was in pursuit. Yells of rage and the pounding of heavy boots followed them down the tunnel.

Emily glanced over her shoulder as she ran. She knew they didn't have much of a head start, but if they could just get through that door into the kitchen they'd be safe. There would be people around preparing food for the day's functions. Holworthy wouldn't be able to harm them in public.

Suddenly Drift stopped in front of a metal door. *This has to be it!* Emily thought. But something was wrong. Drift yelped and sprang back. Jack grabbed the handle and pulled the door open. Then he cursed in pain.

Searing heat, leaping flames and choking smoke all began to pour into the tunnel.

Scott dragged Jack away and kicked the door shut.

'What's going on?' Emily gasped. 'Is the manor on fire?'

Jack blew on his hands, which had been burned on the scalding metal. 'The tunnel comes out in the fireplace. They must have lit a fire in it today!'

With her heart in free-fall, Emily turned to search for another escape route. But she was looking straight at the barrel chest of Dan Holworthy. He was brandishing the spade above his head.

'So this tunnel comes out in the kitchen fireplace, does it?' he laughed. 'Looks like it really *is* my lucky day. They're doing a hog-roast for a big Tudor banquet today. You've got no escape!'

Holworthy laughed again. But he stopped as Drift shot forward and bit his shin. He yelled and lashed out with the spade. He missed Drift, but caught Emily's arm as she dived to pull him out of the way.

Emily cried out and jumped back holding her arm.

'I've had enough of you lot!' Holworthy bellowed. He began swinging the spade round at random, coming closer and closer. 'You won't get away again!'

Scott could see no way out. They were caught between an impassable fire and a madman with a lethal weapon. He pushed the others behind him and covered his head, waiting for the blows to fall. But just when he thought it was all over, Holworthy made a *humph* noise and staggered backwards. He took three steps and swayed from side to side, before toppling over like a mighty oak tree felled by a chainsaw.

Someone had crept up behind him and hit him over the head with a silver candlestick.

And this time it *was* Theo Jarvis!

Theo grinned at the friends, then held up the

candlestick and shone his torch beam on it. 'Seemed appropriate somehow,' he said casually. 'Annie Cuttance betrayed Thomas Pendragon over a stolen silver candlestick. And now this candlestick has saved Pendragon's treasure from being flogged off at a car boot sale.' He shook Holworthy by the shoulder to make sure he was still out cold. 'Help me tie up this dude before he comes round and starts his spade-juggling act again.'

Scott looked at Theo and then at Jack and Emily, trying to catch up with what had just happened. One second they were about to be roasted alive and/or flattened by a spade, the next, Theo was acting as if he'd just strolled by for a chat. It was like suddenly flipping TV channels. Scott knew Theo was a laid-back kind of guy, but this was beyond cool.

Lost for words, Scott helped to bind Holworthy's hands behind his back. Meanwhile, Jack kicked the spade out of reach in case Holworthy woke up.

But Emily just glowered at Theo. 'You stole the Pendragon compass!'

Theo looked up from tying Holworthy's ankles together. 'Well, I wouldn't call it *stealing*, exactly.'

'What would you call it then?' Emily snapped. 'You took it from the wreck without permission.'

Theo grinned and shrugged. 'It's a fair cop. But, like I said, not really stealing. This compass belongs to my family.' And with that, Theo reached into the pocket of his surfer shorts and pulled out a small octagonal brass and silver object.

Scott, Emily and Jack all gazed at the compass resting in Theo's palm. He must have polished it because it glinted softly in the light of his torch. 'Your family?' they repeated in unison.

Theo laughed. 'Nice harmonies, guys! You thought of forming a band? But yes, I'm a Pendragon. On my mum's side, of course. Jarvis is my dad's name. Mum's great-grandfather lost Pendragon Manor and all the family money in gambling debts. We've lived in London for ages, but last year I thought it would be cool to come back and work in Castle Key, near the old ancestral home.'

'But *why* did you nick the compass?' Scott asked.

Theo shrugged. 'When I heard you guys talking about it, I thought it'd be good sport to see if I could find the hoard of treasure my ancestors left behind. So first thing the next morning, I took the jeep down the old track to Pirate Cove, paddled out in a kayak and dived to the wreck. I found the compass dangling from the skeleton's neck just like you said.'

'And you left this behind?' Emily took the Scooby-Doo compass from her bag.

'Oh, yeah!' Theo laughed. 'That was just a spur of the moment thing. These toy compasses came as freebies with an order of Scooby-Doo buckets and spades I was unpacking the other day. I found it in my pocket when

I was changing into my wetsuit. I thought it could be like a calling card. My nickname was always Shaggy at school.' He patted his mop of sun-bleached hair. 'Can't think why!'

Theo finished tying up Holworthy and stood up, although still hunched over under the low roof. 'My turn for a question now. How did you guys figure out where the hiding place was without the compass?'

'We found the concretion that you chipped off and we took plaster casts,' Emily said. 'Then we figured out that *Cross My Heart* meant the family tomb.'

'I figured that part out, actually,' Jack chipped in.

'Awesome!' Theo said. 'It took me ages to work it out, and I had the compass. I found the chapel and the tomb last night but I couldn't get it to open so I gave up. Tell you the truth, I got a bit spooked. I thought I'd heard footsteps when I first came into the chapel, but I couldn't see anyone.'

Jack grinned. 'That was me!'

Theo laughed in surprise. 'That explains it! I was imagining all kinds of ghosts and ghouls. So I decided to head back and try again in the daylight. When I got to the chapel this morning I noticed the side of the Pendragon tomb was open a crack, so I pushed it and it slid back. I climbed in and followed the tunnel. I'd just come across the treasure when I heard a kerfuffle down here, so I followed the noise – and found our man here about to splat you lot on the head with a spade. Who is he anyway? He definitely needs to chill out a bit.'

'Yeah, you could say that,' Scott laughed. 'He has a bit of an anger management issue.'

Emily couldn't help liking Theo, but she wasn't quite ready to forgive him for stealing the compass. 'We still found the smugglers' hoard first,' she told him firmly. 'As long as you admit that, it's OK!'

Theo Jarvis held up his hands and grinned. 'You guys beat me fair and square! Now that we've got that straight, I guess we'd better call the police about our prisoner here. I think he's coming round.'

The next morning, Emily, Scott, Jack and Drift were at Stone Cottage when D. I. Hassan called to update them on the case. To their surprise, Theo Jarvis was with him.

They all sat in the living room and Aunt Kate brought in a tray of tea and scones.

'The current owners of the Pendragon Estate have decided not to press any charges against Theo,' the Detective Inspector explained, taking a sip of tea and smoothing down the ends of his moustache. 'After all, Theo has agreed to return the compass, and nothing was taken from the hoard of contraband in the tunnel. The compass will be put on display at Pendragon Manor. They'll auction off the rest of the old contraband to various museums, but they've agreed that a large portion of the profits should go to the descendants of Thomas Pendragon.'

'Which includes yours truly,' Theo said with a grin. 'They're giving me enough to set up my own surf school in Carrickstowe. Sweet, eh?'

'They've also asked me to give you three this, as a reward for finding the Pendragon hoard.' D. I. Hassan sounded disapproving. He didn't really agree with encouraging the friends in their undercover investigations. He took two bottles covered in dust and shreds of spider web out of a bag and placed them on the coffee table.

Scott picked one up and read the label. 'Brandy? Erm, thanks, but we're not old enough to drink it!'

'Perhaps Aunt Kate could use it for her Christmas cake next year,' Jack laughed.

'I wasn't suggesting you drink it!' D. I. Hassan said. 'Look at the vintage.'

'1756,' Scott read out loud.

Theo laughed. 'That stuff was old even when Pendragon smuggled it back from France on the *Mermaid*.'

'Those bottles are worth hundreds of pounds!' D. I. Hassan explained. 'You can keep them, or sell them and invest the money.'

'What happened to Holworthy?' Scott asked.

D. I. Hassan smiled. 'We've suspected Daniel

Holworthy of dealing in stolen property and bootleg goods for a long time, but we could never find enough evidence to charge him. Couldn't work out where he was storing the stuff. He's helping us with our enquiries now. Giving us a lot of leads to organized crime rings.'

Emily took a scone, fed half of it to Drift and munched happily. Everything had turned out perfectly. Joe Gordon had gained lots of great publicity from the lecture at Pendragon Manor and had already got another contract to salvage gold bullion from a wreck off the coast of Florida. Kelly Mann had received a call from the BBC to say they wanted to go ahead with the documentary film based on her research. Jack was already planning his starring role! And, best of all, Operation Compass was successfully resolved and neatly written up in her notebook.

There was a ring at the doorbell and Aunt Kate hurried off to answer it. When she came back she handed a brochure to Emily. 'That was Rick Trevithick,' she said. 'He thought you'd like to see this leaflet about a new jellyfish exhibit at Sea World in Carrickstowe. Since you're so interested in jellyfish, he said.'

Jack and Scott stared at Emily. '*Jellyfish?*' they chorused. 'Since when have you been interested in jellyfish?'

Emily blushed. 'You don't know *everything* about me!'

Aunt Kate gave her a smile. 'Every girl's entitled to

have some secrets, isn't that right, Emily?'

Scott shot his great-aunt a sideways glance. She should know! He still hadn't figured out how Aunt Kate knew so much about codes and spying, but he suspected she had a great many more secrets apart from knowing how to make the perfect scone.

—

After the others had gone, Aunt Kate asked the boys to fetch in a basket of logs for the fire.

Scott was about to try to get out of it when he remembered his Shark Deal again. 'I'll go,' he told Jack. 'You sit down.'

Jack barred his way out of the door. 'I don't know why you're being so nice to me lately. But can you please *stop*? It's giving me the creeps!'

Scott thought for a minute. Surely he'd paid off the basking shark for not eating him by now. 'With pleasure!' he laughed, handing Jack the log basket. He threw himself down on the sofa and stretched out comfortably as Jack sighed and stomped off to get the wood. School would be starting next week and they'd be going home to London. They'd miss Castle Key, but they'd be back again soon.

And who knew what adventures lay in store for them next time?

Author's Note

The Carters, including the King of Prussia, really were a famous family of Cornish smugglers. Black Joan, Cruel Copinger and Battling Bill were also real people. However, Thomas Pendragon and Mad George Mann were invented for the purposes of this story.

Don't miss the next exciting mystery in the
Adventure Island series

THE MYSTERY
OF THE INVISIBLE SPY

Available now!

Read on for a special preview
of the first chapter.

One

Ambush!

Emily Wild checked her watch.
The boys were late.

Scott and Jack's train – the 10.06 from London to Penzance – had been due to arrive at Carrickstowe Station seventeen minutes ago. Allowing five minutes to get their bikes off the train and another ten to cycle through town, they should be crossing the causeway from the mainland to Castle Key precisely *now*!

Emily leaned back against the trunk of the willow tree and felt the ridges of warm bark through her t-shirt. The broad branch made a perfect observation post. Camouflaged by leafy fronds, you could monitor everyone entering or leaving the island across the causeway. Emily lowered the binoculars and wrote in the notebook propped open on her knees: *TESCO delivery van, 15.15*. That guy was running late too. Mrs Roberts at Lilac Cottage had her shopping delivered every Thursday afternoon and it usually arrived at ten past three.

'Maybe there's a traffic jam in Carrickstowe,' she said. 'What do you think, Drift?'

Drift was inside the hollow tree playing chicken with two very annoying squirrels. Every time he got close, they scurried up to a higher branch, taunting him and pulling faces. Drift perked one ear – the white one with brown spots – at Emily's words. He didn't know what she was saying, of course, but he was a very good listener.

'Jack's probably stopped to buy some sweets at the station kiosk,' Emily told him. 'Or they've got into a row over the quickest route to the causeway.' Emily didn't have any brothers or sisters herself, so when she'd first met Scott and Jack Carter she'd been a bit taken aback that arguing was their normal mode of communication. But that was a year ago and she was used to it now. Since then, they'd found buried treasure, discovered a new species of dinosaur, rescued a film star and tracked down a legendary cursed ruby, to name but a few of their adventures together.

Emily lifted the binoculars again, screwing up her eyes against the glare. The sun was sparkling off the waves in the channel between the island and the mainland; it bleached the sails of the yachts to a dazzling white and glinted off the wings of the gulls as they swooped. The tarmac road across the causeway shimmered in the heat haze. A green and yellow bus lumbered across, followed by a small silver car.

Emily did a double take. She cross-checked the registration number against yesterday's records. Yes, that was the same Ford Fiesta she'd seen three times in the last three days. She was pretty sure it didn't belong to anyone local. The driver was a young man on his own and Emily had never seen him talking to anyone. She'd spotted his car in some odd locations too. Once he was driving slowly along a moorland track near the quarry. And twice she'd seen him parked in a lay-by near Westward Beach. She was sure he'd sped off as soon as he noticed her glance in his direction as she cycled past.

Highly suspicious, Emily thought as she recorded the sighting in her notebook.

She picked up the binoculars again and, at last, she spotted two cyclists. Jack was in front, head down and legs pumping manically on the pedals of his BMX bike. Scott followed at a more leisurely pace, his floppy brown hair flying back in the breeze. A year older than Jack, Scott was more laid-back and – he liked to think – way cooler than his brother. Emily giggled. With their bulky backpacks, the boys looked like giant snails, carrying their homes on their backs.

She waited until the boys had left the causeway and were on the island road not far from the willow tree. Then she dangled her legs from the branch and dropped to the ground. Calling softly for Drift to follow, she commando-crawled through the bracken to the edge of the road.

'Stand and deliver!' she shouted as she leaped out of the undergrowth.

'Aggghhh!' Jack yelled, slamming his brakes on so hard they squealed. He'd been daydreaming about the gallons of ice-cold Coke he was going to knock back as soon as he got to Stone Cottage. Knowing Aunt Kate, she'd have some awesome cakes waiting for them too. Then they'd head off to The Lighthouse to see Emily and Drift. He had it all worked out. Then, all of a sudden, he was being set upon by a mugger and some kind of ferocious beast – quite possibly a mountain lion.

'Look what you're doing!' Scott shouted, almost crashing into him.

Jack opened his eyes and realized the ambushers were only Emily and Drift. He staggered onto the wide verge, dropped his bike against the hedge and with arms outstretched, keeled over backwards onto his rucksack in the long grass, sending up a cloud of fluffy white dandelion seeds. Drift bounced onto his stomach and licked his face in joyful greeting, as the seeds wafted around them like miniature parachutes.

'We saw you coming a mile off!' Jack spluttered through the tsunami of dog drool.

Scott flopped down next to him. 'Yeah, we were just *pretending* to be surprised!' he said, laughing as Drift belly-flopped onto his chest.

'Of course you were!' Emily laughed. She couldn't *stop* laughing, in fact, as the boys wriggled around like upturned beetles, pinned down by their heavy backpacks. When they finally managed to sit up she greeted them both with an awkward high-five-slash-hug. She quickly pulled away in case they thought she was being soppy. 'So what took you so long?' she asked. 'No, don't tell me. Jack stopped for sweets and then you couldn't agree which way to come.'

Jack stared at Emily and then at the pack of toffees he'd just pulled from his backpack. She was right! He *had* felt a bit peckish when they got off the train and had made a quick detour for emergency provisions. Then Scott refused to take a brilliant short-cut, just because it would involve lifting their bikes over a locked gate. Had Emily developed mind-reading powers since they'd last seen her?

Scott swigged from a bottle of water. 'You must've had your spies out watching us, Em!'

'I didn't need to!' Emily laughed. 'You two are just so predictable.'

'No, we're not!' Scott and Jack protested.

'Anyway, on the subject of spies,' Emily said, switching into a serious tone all of a sudden. 'I've spotted one.' She paused dramatically and looked from Jack to Scott and back again. 'Right here on Castle Key!'

THE ADVENTURE CONTINUES
Secret agent tests
•
Character profiles
•
Hidden codes
•
Exclusive blogs
•
Cool downloads
DO YOU HAVE
WHAT IT TAKES?
Find out at
www.adventureislandbooks.com
Illustrations © Roy Knipe

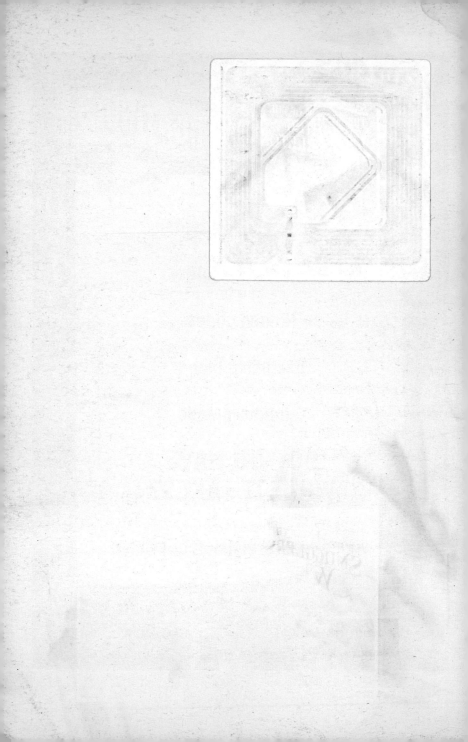